A Crude Tool
for Self-Decapitation

by
Mike Bujniewicz

To Everyone I ever said I'd dedicate this book to.

(I'm a man of my word,
but I never said I'd do it by name.)

Chapter 1

Atypicalmorning

Sitting in the dark of my basement, smoking a cigarette, and staring at an unmoving desktop—I start to contemplate what to do. In the dim light of the computer monitor, I see something scurry across the floor out of the corner of my eye. I jump back in my chair, rolling it into the futon behind me, and scan the floor in search of the creature as I nervously puff away.

A bug?

It looked bigger than any bug I've ever seen.

Rat?

Mouse?

No, too small for that.

Cockroach?

Maybe, but that's unlikely; the only cockroach I've ever seen in here is the one I nearly attack every time I see that fuckin' Orkin commercial.

There it is, almost invisible, over by the TV stand.

What the hell is it? And more importantly, why does it have the same stealth technology as a predator?

As my eyes adjust, I start to make out its shape. Somehow—despite the fact that it's about the size of your stereotypical cockroach, and looks like an obese praying mantis—I know it's a termite.

Termite? What the fuck are you thinking?

I don't know.

Termite, yea, maybe if what you mean by Termite is a creature from the planet Term.

Hey, you're not helping the situation at hand, and besides this is my dream so I'll call it what I want.

Wait! This is a dream! Why am I talking to myself when I can do anything I want?

And when's the last time you had a dream that logic worked in?

Never, but I blame you and your damn logic for that.

You mean you and your damn logic.

Mother fucker! This is not the time to be arguing with myself, let alone arguing semantics. There's Termites to deal with.

Fuck, me!

Termites!

Now that I mention it they're all over, literally coming out of the woodwork.

I get up out of the chair and poke the original Termite with my cigarette. An almost deafening pop splatters the room with glowing green goo, and fills the air with the taste and smell of chemicals.

Holy shit!

All a-sudden the room is lit by the light of a crap load of nonexistent candles, like some sorta color filter straight out of Nosferatu. I see what seems like thousands of Termites swarming around me, preparing to enact their revenge. Just as the mass of them is about to devour my feet, I hop back onto the chair.

We stare each other down for a long moment.

Waking up for just long enough to look across the room at the alarm clock, I roll over and fall back asleep.

Next thing I know, I'm driving my friend Ferris's car with his girlfriend Tracy riding shotgun. Before I even have a moment to consider how odd it is that I'm actually driving, Tracy calls out in a drunken slur, "Stopere Iged pee!"

I park in a handicap space, since the road has transformed into an empty Walmart parking lot in the short moment I wasn't watching it. Tracy struggles getting out of the car. She has to put much more effort into simply lifting her legs than any normal human being, even a drunk one, should. Once she finally manages to get her feet out of the car and on the ground—she proceeds to slowly stumble toward a giant bird bath, which is slightly taller than the building itself.

What the Fuck!

She's completely naked!

Now I would be lying if I said I'd never imagined her naked before, but seeing it now makes me lose a certain degree of interest in ever seeing it in reality. I would think that in a dream she would be idealized, but it's quite the opposite. She almost looks like a used condom: sticky, translucent, and all scrunched up as if making a futile attempt to keep her soul from dripping out.

She climbs onto the first tier of the structure with a relative amount of ease, but has a little trouble climbing up onto the second level. Once on top, she immediately squats and starts to fill that portion with her piss, but the plastic structure begins to fail and she quickly loses what little balance she had.

I get out of the car and rush over to her while she falls, but as soon as I get close her head bashes into the ground at my feet, somehow only stunning her. I'm frozen in shock for a moment but quickly regain my senses, pick her up, carry her back to the car, and lay her down in the passenger seat.

As I start the car, an unusually dark-skinned man appears out of nowhere and taps on the driver-side window. I crack the window and he asks, "How much fo' dat fine white ho ya got dare?"

I give him a blank stare of surprise for a second then snap out of it noticing a couple cars pulling up behind me.

Fuck this shit! I'm not stickin' around here.

I gun it and get the fuck outta there. When I look back to see if anyone's following us—I notice that not only has Tracy recovered from her fall, but she's managed to teleport into the back seat where she and Ferris, (Where'd he come from?), are making out intensely.

I continue to drive the car, without the convenience of headlights, in what has become a pitch black environment. Bushes and small trees fill up the no longer existing road, and the car begins to plow through them.

CUT TO:

The bottom of a heavily forested hill.

After a great deal of cracking and crashing noises—I watch us ride what is left of the car, which now looks something like the world's most ghetto pair of jet skis dragging a couch that has Ferris and Tracy on it: still ceaselessly making out.

Once we come to a complete stop, the two of them finally pause to catch their breath.

Ferris looks around and yells, "What the fuck did you do to my car Alden?!"

I step off the junk pile and exclaim, "You knew damn well you shouldn't have let me drive!"

The discussion ends there, and we all walk through an empty field for a moment before arriving at a house where we hear some sorta party going on. We go inside and are enthusiastically greeted by a man; who judging by his pencil thin mustache and greasy black hair, which hangs somewhere in limbo just shy of becoming a mullet, can be nothing other than a sleazy porn producer.

Upon surveying the room, this immediately makes sense, because calling it a party is a gross understatement of the orgy we just walked into. It looks as if the sets of a hundred porn movies have all converged on each other. All the stereotypical porn characters are there just scrambled-up: schoolgirls are being taken from behind by cowboys, plumbers are sucked off by secretaries, lonely housewives sixty-nine farmer daughters while they are both being fucked by football players, delivery boys give rim-jobs to naughty nurses, and all these acts bleed together linked by the penetration of one orifice or another. In literally no time at all, Ferris and Tracy immerse themselves in this orgy while I just sit by the door smoking a joint.

I spend a few minutes watching Ferris work the room like a slick cross between Jesus and Don Juan—getting numbers from and fooling around with nearly every girl there, even as they are railed by faceless men. All the while, Tracy is gang-banged in the corner—never having less than two cocks in her at any given moment, and gradually beginning to look like she'd bathed in mayonnaise. Having had enough, I decide to leave.

I make my way out the door muttering, "This shit is too fucked up for me."

Outside, I walk down the street: finishing the joint, flicking the roach into the road, and lighting a cigarette along the way. I turn left at the first corner I get to and see a cop car parked right there on the side of the road. Two cops sit inside the car munching on donuts. They watch me in their mirrors as I walk past them and make my way down the block.

Suddenly, they call out, "Hey," and I quick turnaround only to see a couple of punk kids approach the driver's side window. They all jibber on about some promotional trading cards meant to make kids more comfortable approaching cops. Realizing that it isn't a good idea to steal a car with cops right there, I backtrack to the orgy.

When I reenter the house, things have quieted down considerably; only a few stray clusters of people are still going at it while the majority of them have passed out in piles around the room. I look for Ferris and Tracy among the bodies, but they've already been entirely absorbed into these indiscernible heaps of flesh. I forget all about them though, when I see a girl from the local bar I've been known to frequent. Aside from myself, she is the only person in the room who is not drenched or at least stained with some sort of bodily fluid, which makes her unforced and natural beauty stick out all the more. In deep contrast to the mass-produced plastic whores in the room, she has an almost tomboyish look to her: with her chin length brown hair, a T-Shirt of some indie band I've never heard of, and cargo pants. Recognizing me, she smiles and makes her way across the room as if she is above and oblivious to all the depravity around us. We talk for a moment in fast forward, and it seems to go pretty well.

I've had the hots for her awhile now, but she's never appeared in a dream before.

Come on dream-sex! If there ever was the time for my dream consciousness mind-powers to activate it's now!

The progress of time returns to normal just as I lean in to kiss her, but she puts a hand on my shoulder and gently pushes me away saying, "I'm sorry sweety, I thought you knew I had a boyfriend."

I bow my head in defeat for the briefest of moments, and when I look up—in the blink on an eye Ferris appears, she grabs him, and they start making out.

FUCK THIS DREAM!

Opening my eyes, thankful to be out of that bastard of a dream, I look at the alarm clock again.

Plenty of time for sleep.

Stretching out, I roll over a few times and frustratedly mumble, "Can't even control my damn lucid dreams!"

I close my eyes.

Come on now.

Dream-sex this time.

Think.

Who?

Hot gothic chick.

Black latex, or vinyl, or whatever dress.

Named after a common household pet.

I'm in the middle of a battlefield, or maybe playing a <u>Battlefield</u> game, it is hard for me to distinguish between the two. Behind enemy lines I closely follow a squad of three troops. I pull out my pistol and get a bead on the closest one. I pull out my knife and charge. Slicing at the first one...

I don't even bother to look at the fucking clock or open my eyes.
Come on! At least let me kill something.

I'm sitting shotgun at a checkpoint in what judging by the horizon of sand and smell of shit in the air can only be a Middle Eastern country. Two soldiers order me and the driver out at gun point. We get out and in a thick Arabic accent one of the soldiers tells us, "Our methods may seem strange, but we get our job done."
One of them takes a crate out of the back of our truck and boots it across the road then grabs a gas can out of the broken crate. He takes it over to another car and pours some into a jug of milk. As he turns toward us the milk jug bursts into flames. We all rush to the middle of the road and I grab the gas can. The soldier violently takes it back and puts the cap on.
He leans in closer, looks me in the eye, and says, "We wouldn't want any milk to get in here!"

Now that was just fucking weird.
I look over at the alarm clock again.
Still got an hour, maybe I'll actually get some good sleep.

I close my eyes and put a pillow over them.

It feels very familiar. A million events occur in fast forward. None of them stick out or register at all, but it feels as if they've all happened before. The fast forwarding stops and I'm standing on top of a bullet train. In an instant, I work out an infinitely complex and unintelligible math problem. I laugh maniacally as explosions ignite all around me.

Somehow, I know this is the end of the world, and I'm responsible for it.

I jump up in bed, covered in a cold sweat.
Why do I never grasp any more of that dream?
I look over at the alarm clock.
Still 15 minutes till it goes off.
Yawning, I grab my glasses off the table next to the futon, put them on, and grab my lighter and a cigarette. As I light that smoke I pull my folder of masturbation material out from under a nearby stack of notebooks. I arrange 5 or 6 pictures in order from the least to most arousing.

Getting myself off, I weave a story in my mind taking me from girl to girl. As always, it ends before I'm able to make it to the last or even the next to last picture. I put the folder away just in time to get up, and turn off the alarm before it can make a sound.

Chapter 2

The Introduction
by Alden Baird

I suppose here, as the second chapter, is the best place for my introduction. After all, if it was just The Introduction many a reader wouldn't bother with it and if it was the first chapter it might as well have just been The Introduction. It would've ended up like the aborted child of some pro-choice whore, its existence only acknowledged by some deranged extremists. Here, however, in Chapter 2, what would have been literary waste can be given a little charisma thanks to a simple highlight and click.

As you read, or rather continue to read, there are some things that you should keep in mind. The most important of these is that if you find yourself reading arrangements of words like:

> "If you enjoyed the movie <u>Fight Club</u> the only reason you could've had any anger on 9-11 is because you were angry that the terrorists were as motivated as members of Project Mayhem while you could only muster up enough will to have a

> poor excuse for a Fight Club in a friend's
> backyard. They beat you to it America, and you're
> such sore losers you can't bring yourselves to give
> them their well earned props and virgin slaves."

know that I do not necessarily condone or take seriously any given thought. I've often told people that if they're taking me seriously more often than not they shouldn't be, and if they aren't... well, they probably should be.

Also, and I'll put it plainly. If I tell you to kill yourself or kill/destroy anyone/thing, or in any way make that sound like a good idea, don't go out and do it. If I tell you not to do anything, even heroin, don't not go out and try/do/continue-to-do it on my account. I don't want you to end up like someone who lives by the code of a self-help book or some murderous religious fanatic, as most of the religious tend to be, on account of any words written by anyone—even those of myself or some tripped out prophet from ancient times, reformed Jew or otherwise.

In reading this, you are legally bound to take everything written here with at least one of those little paper packets, if not a shaker full, of salt. Though I don't think that is actually legally binding, if you don't or are unwilling to follow that suggestion this book would be better used to slowly cut through your own neck until you have decapitated yourself, and last I checked paper cuts weren't very efficient at getting through bone.

But before I go off any further on a nonsensical rant about literature, religion, society, and/or any other random thing I'll end this, get back to my basement where I had just woken up for the day, and let those thoughts come on their own, if they do at all.

Chapter 3

Out with the Phlegm

I grab my wireless keyboard and sit in my chair lighting another cigarette. I check my downloads and stop sharing most of what finished in my sleep, if you can call it that. Seems like it was a far too tiring to be sleep.

What now?

I puff on the cigarette for a moment, trying to sift through the haze of dream fragments and morning wood fantasies that keeps me from remembering what I was going to do.

Homework for today's class?

No, I'm a procrastinator, but not that big of one.

I think it had something to do with the computer, but I can't remember what it was.

Giving up on remembering, I get up and put out my cigarette. I grab the previous days' socks off my foot rest and examine them.

Still white for the most part, and only slightly starched in the toes from sweat. They'll do for another day. Maybe two if I'm lucky, or lazy, or both.

I put them on in a few yawns then smell my fingers.

That's the smell of socks and feet alright!

Were you expecting something else?

No, but you never know, someday there might be a pleasant surprise. Besides, if the first thing you smell in the morning, aside from the cigarettes that are gradually killing your sense of smell, is feet—you tend to be less self-conscious about how the rest of you smells. It's all spring fresh compared to feet, any feet. Not that I have any qualms with feet, they tend to be very useful and an unappreciated day-to-day necessity, but you won't find me begging and drooling for a stinky foot job. That is unless you're some sorta kinky dominatrix getting off on that, but even then I'd probably just be making myself imagine that you walk around on a pair of tits.

On that somewhat disturbing note, I begin to look through a pile of recently worn shirts that reside on my futon for the time being. I find one I haven't worn for a week or so, that doesn't have any noticeable stains on it, then put it on while computing how long I've been wearing this particular pair of pants for.

One...

Two...

Three...

Four days, that's not too bad. They've got at least another day or two left in 'em.

Filling my pockets—I grab my cellphone, wallet, keys, PDA, and a pen. I make my way upstairs and say, "Hi," to my dad, who says the same as I squint and allow my eyes to adjust to the sunlit kitchen. Making my way to the bathroom, I pass him sitting in his usual spot at the head of the kitchen table.

I close the door behind me then unzip, pull out, and start peeing. The pee struggles to get out at first, but once the last bit of goo from my morning recreation plops in the water, I'm pissing full stream. I almost piss all over the floor as I lean forward to hack up the first bit in what will be a large amount of morning phlegm. I finish pissing and feed the toilet a couple more hacks before flushing it with my foot. I wash my hands in the sink and hack up a little more. One glob lands too high on the sink for the water to reach so I help it along with a splash of water as it drips down then repeat the entire process. I dry my hands slightly on the towel and run the excess water through my hair to reactivate yesterday's gel then wash and dry my hands one last time, and make one more hack into the toilet for good measure before I exit the room.

Upon reentering the kitchen, I pull out another cigarette and light it.

My dad says, "You look tired." and I respond with an affirming grunt.

No shit, I'm tired, I just woke up and as usual since I didn't give myself the twelve plus hours of sleep I need to feel refreshed I didn't sleep well at all.

He moves the ashtray from its usual resting place on his right to the other side of the table, so I don't have to reach for it, but mainly so his coffee cup is not in danger of being tainted by any stray ash from my cigarette. I finish smoking the cigarette without being bothered to make any half awake small talk.

I head back down into the basement and grab my bag of books, notebooks, and folders for school. Setting the bag on the floor by my dresser I grab a stick of deodorant and apply it to my armpits. I sniff one pit as I put the stick down then grab my Axe deodorant spray and give my feet and pelvic region a spritz. I grab my bag, turn off the lights, and start to head back upstairs practically tripping over a clothes basket that has made its way into my usual path and now across the room with my trip/kick. I push the basket to a less intrusive place before continuing on my way up into the kitchen.

Damn it! Forgot to put my shoes on.

I toss the bag by my chair at the kitchen table then go back downstairs, and past the washer and dryer. I stop at the large old fashioned sink, made of cement made to look like metal, and lean over it hacking up phlegm uncontrollably for a minute—as it keeps filling up my throat, making me feel like I'm going to suffocate.

Now why the hell did I come back down here?

I sit on the edge of my futon, puzzled and frustrated by my forgetfulness as I scan the room.

Nothing on the table.

The computer?

Nope, but I think I forgot something I had wanted to do on it earlier.

Let's see…………………………………………………..
…………………………………………………..oh, shoes!

I grab my beat up old high-tops, put them on, and stare at the computer for a minute—trying to remember what I had wanted to do again—before I give up and head back upstairs. In the kitchen, I grab a soda out of the fridge. I crack it open as I make my way into the living room, and sit down on the folded-in love seat that doubles as my dad's bed at night. Fox News is on as usual, since despite the hundreds of channels that come with digital cable my dad pretty much watches only Fox News, sports, and

DVDs—most of which Bill O'Reilly and his colleagues would quickly boycott and attempt to get banned if they knew the movies existed.

Fair and balanced news my ass, what a horrible joke. It's the polar opposite of the stereotypical exaggeration that the media is liberal and Jew run. Apparently, having a couple of soft spoken people pretending to be liberals, so they can be over powered by assholish, virtually deaf conservatives, makes it fair and balanced. I've seen less one-sided and more intelligent conversations on Jerry Springer than I do on Fox News half the time.

Oh to be on Fox News, the only network where someone who is pretending to be a respectable journalist will ask a person the really important loaded questions like:

> "Based on the way that you treat anyone that disagrees with you, combined with your settled-out-of-court phone-sex scandal, some people might believe that you might have been molested as a child, and in turn may currently molest children, and you are taking your guilt and shame out on everyone around you both sexually and verbally."

Wait, question?

That was a period thus making it a statement, or so I was taught nearly everyday in elementary school as part of the annoying grammar work we did on the overhead projector.

Oh wait!

I forgot, it takes awhile for even a professional reputation killer to load a question, but the question comes:

"What would you say to them?"

What the hell kinda question is that!?!

Say to them when, about what, and under what circumstances?

Did they just sneeze?

Bless them.

Did they just burp?

Bellllch!

Or did they just fart?

Doorknob.

Maybe they shat their pants.

It happens to the best of us.

To even acknowledge the question would be ridiculous, but walking out would somehow justify the question itself.

What a terrorist! Terrifying those poor Jews who run the media.

Aren't we on their side, or are the Jews doomed to be nothing more then the historical scapegoat for 21st century U.S. imperialism?

Shall we purge the world of the heathens?

They terrorize Jews.

Now us too.

9-11.

We must kill them oil.

Ahehem, in closing, 9-11.

I finish my soda, in a second gulp, after being pulled out of that jumbled mess of thoughts by Peter Francis Gerraci who pops on the TV to profess his ability to help us all go bankrupt.

> *An annoying man,*
> *but one with a dream,*
> *of a better world,*
> *where everyone was bankrupt.*

Saint Peter Francis Gerraci

That's probably what his tombstone will read. The birth and death dates omitted due to a controversy over how long he's really been dead for, and whether or not he really was alive to begin with.

I walk through the kitchen and throw the empty can away, pausing to grab a kleenex, blow my nose, and give the regular garbage can a couple good hacks of phlegm to go with the kleenex. I light a cigarette and put it in the ashtray as I grab another soda out of the fridge and crack it open. On the news they start talking about a suicide bombing in Iraq.

I turn to my dad and say, "Jeez, does a day go by without that happening?"

Setting down his coffee and getting up to get a cigarette from his den, he responds, "We should just pull out our troops and let them all kill each other."

"Yeah, we should've never taken Saddam out of power. Seems like they need a ruthless dictator to keep them in line."

He chuckles saying, "You might be right." then lights the cigarette he'd gotten and changes the subject, "You know, you watch a movie you haven't watched in years, and it's like watching it for the first time again."

"Yeah."

"I watched <u>Casino</u> last night."

"Great movie, haven't seen it in years, though."

"Yeah... those old guys really worked 'em over with those bats at the end."

"Yeah, Joe Pesci..."

"And his brother." my dad adds.

I put out my cigarette, and he brushes a couple stray flakes of ash off the table before saying, "You know how many people must be buried out in that desert?"

"Oh, a shitload, I'm sure."

"Yeah, and there's really no way you could find those bodies without some sorta detector."

"I'm sure you could solve a lot of unsolved murders that way."

"Yeah."

I finish my soda and throw it away.

"The other..." he stops for a moment as I hack up a little phlegm in the garbage can. "The other part I really got a kick out of was DeNiro with the pen."

"Oh yeah," I say, "that's one of my favorite parts out of any of those gangster movies."

"He really does a number on that guy."

"Yeah, just like that one deleted scene from <u>Natural Born Killers</u>."

"Oh, where uh, where Woody Harrelson kills Ashley Judd with a pencil?"

"Yeah, in the courtroom."

"They should've left that part in."

"Yeah." I agree.

He puts out his cigarette saying, "You'd be surprised how much of what they're saying you miss when you don't have the subtitles on."

Heading toward the bathroom, I nod.

He continues, "Especially when you watch some of those British movies, and they talk in that damn Cockney accent."

As I hack up a little more phlegm in the toilet he mentions some other movies, most of which I don't catch.

Damn allergies.

I return to the kitchen and pet one of the stupid cats sitting on the kitchen table. I blame them for my phlegm ignoring the fact that the pack, if not two packs, of cigarettes I smoke a day might have more to do with it.

My dad goes on, saying, "You know, if you ever run out of things to watch, I got tons of DVDs and I'm sure there are quite a few you'd like to see."

"Yeah."

"We don't have to go to Blockbuster to rent anything anymore, that's for sure."

"You probably have a bigger selection than they do, anyways."

"Yeah... you remember that one place we went to..."

Anticipating what he's talking about since we've had the same conversation numerous times, I answer before he can even ask the question, "Video Update!"

"Yeah, they had to have had the worst selection."

"Yeah."

We both look at the clock and see that it's time to leave so he can drop me off at school.

Yes, I'm in my twenties and a college student, but I still have my dad take me to school since I don't drive. Don't even have a license, but I have my reasons, whether they be good or bad.

He asks, "You ready for this?"

"I suppose..." I answer, "as ready as I ever am."

He chuckles as we both put on our jackets. I grab my bag, he puts on his driving/reading glasses, and we make our exit—locking the door behind us. We head out of the yard through the gate to avoid traversing a minefield of dog shit on the way to the car. My dad opens one side of the driveway gate and I take care of the other as he starts up the car.

He backs out of the driveway and I close the gate, struggling for a moment with one of those keychains that it isn't safe to climb mountains with. We use it to help ensure that wind won't blow the gate open. Then, with the gate secured, I get out my last few hacks of morning phlegm and hop into the car.

Chapter 4

Car Ride Paranoia

I put my bag at my feet as I get in the car and brace myself against the door for a ten to fifteen minute waking nightmare of paranoid delusions. I don't buckle up since that act would somehow show my lack of faith in my father's driving skills, which I have every right to have but feel guilty about nonetheless.

Now I wasn't always fearful and paranoid when it came to car rides; initially, my reasons for not driving myself were incredibly simple. For one, I just wanted to avoid having any responsibility whatsoever. Driving would require: buying a car, paying for insurance, paying for gas, and all that. Which in turn would require a job and having a job is something I'm not really suited for. I lack people skills and I'm way too out of shape and weakly built for physical labor, which doesn't leave many options left.

Cars speed by as my dad inches out to pull onto the main road. He whips out making a left turn and is clipped by a truck. We are sent spinning past the median and another car smashes into us. As we come to a stop I look

over at my father's body slumped over the steering wheel.
The airbag slowly inflates, pushing him upright so I can
see into his lifeless eyes.

I shake that image out of my head and repeatedly blink
reality back into my vision as we drive on unharmed.

Where was I?
In the car, still alive.
Not physically!
Oh, thinking about... driving.
I never thought I had enough observational ability to
safely operate a car, at least at times when there is more
than a few other cars and people to worry about crashing
into or running over—killing or maiming in the process.
Then, there's the fact that when I could start legally
driving pretty much coincided with when I started
smoking weed and doing various other drugs on a regular
basis. I knew and know I'd be completely incapable of
operating a vehicle on any drug, even weed. At the time
there was no way I was going to let anything at all,
especially driving, interfere with my drug use.
What's the point in driving to a friend's house when
you can't get high, slam cough syrup, or do whatever else
the internet says will get you high, because you have to be
able to make it home in one piece?

An impatient driver whips out of their driveway in
front of us and we smash into their rear end. Both of the
cars crumple and screech like two massive broken
accordions.

The sudden jerk of my dad's abrupt stop jars me back to reality as the car in front of us gets up to speed and we continue on our way without incident.

At the time, I didn't have the current paranoia and sense of impending doom I now get the moment I enter a car. Every near miss of a crash, swerve in the snow, or comical road-rage induced chase by someone who may or may not have been cut off was laughable to me. No one these days wants to admit they have a fear of death. It's uncool, and would make them a pussy. That's why public speaking beats out death as most people's greatest fear in every poll, but it seems to me that only proves that people are bigger pussies than ever.

I fear death, despite the fact that I used to be one of the people who would have answered public speaking, which I also fear immensely. There should be no shame in it though; everyone fears death in one way or another. Even people who kill themselves are scared of it, but suicide is really the only way to get any sense of control over that fear. Mainly, I fear death because it means the game is over. No restarting from a save or checkpoint. At best maybe starting from scratch again or playing an entirely different game, but that's only if you believe in reincarnation. At this point though, death would mean failure. I know the main character dies at the end of the game, but I want the best ending. Death now would mean missing out on the funnest parts and the coolest cut scenes, but despite that, a large part of me just wants to get to the ending as quickly as possible.

If fearing death makes me a pussy, so be it. Everyone who says they have no fear—whether it be out loud, or with some faggoty ass sticker or what have you—needs to realize that any pussy literal or figurative can destroy any man, even just by proximity.

OH SHIT!

Half a block down the road the traffic light turns yellow and my dad puts the pedal to the floor to beat the light. As we run the now red light a cyclist crosses in front of us and we plow right through them before he slams on the brakes sending me flying through the front windshield.

My head jerks up as if I had nodded off to sleep for a brief moment and I strain my neck to look behind us in the side mirror. There is only an empty road and the red light in the distance.

Didn't driver's ed. teach you to stop for yellow lights not speed through them? And what the fuck is so important that it has you constantly looking off to the left like you see some beautiful woman sunbathing naked in her front yard?

As my dad spaces out looking into someone's front yard, I try and see what it is while he slowly drifts into oncoming traffic. Upon determining that there is absolutely nothing in particular that has grabbed his attention, I turn forward just in time to see a semi-truck crash into us head on.

I roll my eyes as he finally brings his attention back to the road ahead of us.

You know, I have probably imagined thousands of possible accidents over the years, ranging from insignificant to earth shattering, but my morbid fascination with doing this has changed since I never imagined the one that did happen. The scenario just seemed too avoidable to even give it thought.

It was a year or two ago; I woke up to go to school around noon. Lighting my regular morning cigarette I threw away the previous day's pack, grabbed my books, and went up into the kitchen. I saw my dad sleeping on the couch and thought, 'Damn, now I'm going to have to wake him up.' After going through the usual routine in the bathroom and finishing my cigarette I went across the street and bought a fresh pack.

Walking back inside and opening the pack, I noticed an empty glass on the table which I knew must've contained Jack Daniel's or maybe Jim Beam at some point, but I thought nothing of it. I sat around and smoked a couple cigarettes hoping he'd wake up on his own and figuring I'd just go back to sleep if he didn't wake up before I'd be late to my second class. I was about to do just that when he popped up and darted to the bathroom. I got up and positioned myself by my spot at the kitchen table. When he got out of the bathroom I asked him if he wanted to take me to school. He looked somewhat disorientated, but he said he would and I thought to myself, 'He can't be any more drunk than usual.'

But this thought was soon proved to be wrong as the next words I'd say to him would be, "Are you okay?" immediately after the accident.

I watched him stumble to the car, barely able to walk, but I didn't say anything not wanting a belligerent response. As he started driving, I noticed he was swerving quite a bit, but I didn't say anything. I only thought to myself, 'I've driven with him and many other people who were drunk before, I have faith that it'll work out fine.' Someone eager to get away from our swerving car illegally sped past us: crossing the double yellow lines. Seeing this as a challenge of some sort my dad sped up and passed them, but I said nothing—not even, "Take it easy!"

The other driver zoomed past us again and took off weaving through cars at increasing speeds; my dad gave chase with very little hesitation. Still, I said nothing—not even, "Slow down!"

In a matter of seconds, we were going over 100 MPH and a car we couldn't stop for was in our path. Exclaiming, "Oh shit!" in synch with my own thoughts, my dad swerved to the right barely avoiding the car. As he jammed on the brakes he swerved back to left to avoid going off the road. At this point no amount of skill, experience, or even drunken luck could bring the car to a controlled stop. My dad and I, both unbuckled, flew around within the car as it flipped across two lanes of oncoming traffic and into someone's front yard, taking out their brand new mail box along the way. Only a well placed tree stopped the crushed and smashed car right side up.

We were lucky.

We should've been dead as one particularly ineloquent sheriff repeatedly told me at the hospital. Though I wasn't as sure as some family members that I, "...must've had some sort of guardian angel, or someone up there looking out for me," I was sure of one thing. That being, I hoped in the future I wouldn't be silent when speaking up could prevent a lot of trouble, regardless of the possibility of fatalities or not.

For awhile, my fear of motor vehicles never really came to fruition. I was riding a sort of high on life kick, trying to do things that I knew I could end up regretting, mainly because I knew I'd regret not having tried them. I wasn't able to live up to that ideal of non-silence for the most part, but I did however create a strange, sweetly poetic love proclamation to one particular girl.

That was probably one of the most pathetic and humiliating experiences of my life though. I was...

Suddenly, a deer jumps into the road out of nowhere and we swerve avoiding it by careening off the road and into a tree.

Now that one didn't even make sense! We're still on a city street!

Anyhow, it wasn't till about a year after the accident, long after the initial near-death adrenaline wore off when two car related experiences in particular triggered my overwhelming fear of driving—both myself or with any other given person. The first of these seems incredibly minor when sandwiched between the previous accident and the near accident to follow, but it set off something in my mind that made part of me fear going on even a short drive with anyone. The second only served amplify the fear to a most likely unhealthy level.

One day, shortly after my dad had finally gotten his license reinstated, he ordered some broasted chicken from a nearby deli and I went with him to pick it up. I noticed him swerving a little bit and knew that he had been drinking which had me paranoid and desperately holding onto the door as if doing so would somehow make the drive safer.

I asked him, "Are you good to drive?"

He just blew it off saying something like, "Don't worry, it's not like I'm gonna get in a chase or anything."

We made it there and back without incident, but I realized then that even though my dad drank less and drove drunk a lot less the only lesson he'd really learned was not to drive fast and recklessly while drunk. My friend Ferris had also learned a ridiculous, obvious, and much too specific lesson from his first DUI. His lesson was, don't drive drunk... when you're on Xanax.

Which brings me to the second incident, Ferris's second DUI. My sister had desperately wanted to get some pot, so after bar close we went to her dealer's place with his roommate; Ferris did the driving. We were all pretty fucked up, but we made it there fine and proceeded to drink a bunch of beer and wine while we waited for the dealer to get home. After a few calls, the roommate finally got a hold of him and was given the okay to sell us a quarter. We all smoked a bowl together before we left.

Ferris was driving pretty erratically as he made his way to drop us off at home. At every stop sign he would make a rolling stop out into the middle of the intersection then pointlessly look both ways before driving on.

I made a comment along the lines of, "That was one helluva rolling stop." but he cockily blew it off and proceeded on in the same fashion.

He laughed about getting busted and was so cocky about it that he even stopped the car in the middle of the road, in front of the fucking police station. He pointed out to us where they book you and where they hold you while my sister and I both kept on insisting, "Come on man let's go! There's cops around..."

Finally, he started driving again, but at the next intersection there was a cop car going down the other road and Ferris nearly did another rolling stop right into them. He swerved enough to barely miss them; which made the position of the stopped cars give the appearance that he had tried to take a right turn and cut them off.

"...and you almost hit them." I added.

Almost immediately, we heard one of the cops yell out, "Turn off the car!"

Ferris turned it off telling us in a far from reassuring slur, "Don' worra, I've tagen field sobredy tits bafore."

That I knew, but had he ever passed?

Doubtful.

I knew we were fucked and had already futilely tried to stash the weed under my seat, leaving it in plain sight except for the fact that it was under my feet. The cops told us to put our hands where they could see them and we all did. They got our IDs and one of them took Ferris out of the car to give him the standard field sobriety tests while the other got on the radio to check all our records.

My sister asked me, "You think he'll pass?"

With some hesitation, hoping for a miracle, I said with certainty, "No."

She asked a couple more times about that, and the weed. I quietly responded, hoping she'd just shut up since the windows were rolled down. I told her the weed was at my feet and was coming out of the car with me, since I wasn't able to kick it under the seat and wasn't about to let Ferris take the fall for it as well. She expressed her dislike of that idea.

While that was going on in the car, I watched Ferris fail his tests in record time. While being prepped to walk in a straight line he staggered twice before his first step and after two swervy stumbles the cop stopped him, cuffed him, and put him in the backseat of the cop car. A moment later, two cops ordered me out of the car. I proceeded to get out in a very awkward manner, since I was dragging the sack of weed out of the car under my right foot. They told me to turn around and put my hands on the car then began asking if I had anything that they should know about on me.

Seeing that the second cop was shining his light on the ground near the pot, I took my right hand off the car and reached down to pick up the bag saying, "Actually..."

"What's that?" the cop asked as he saw it.

"...I was just about to tell him about that..." I declared as one of them pushed me up against the car, "...That's my sack of weed!!"

They yelled at me to put my hands back on the car as they snagged the bag out from under me. I complied and one cop continued to search me while the other took the weed over to his car. The cop asked what I had on me and I proceeded to list everything off as it was removed from my pockets.

"Keys."

"Wallet."

"Cigarettes."

"Lighter."

"Cellphone."

"Empty pack for the miles."

He checked the rest of my pockets to make sure there was nothing else then cuffed me and forced me into the back of the second cop car. After that, they searched my sister and soon after she disappeared from my sight. I watched them search the car for awhile, appearing to just toss things around randomly. Just when I had lost all interest in what they were doing, one of them walked over to me asking if we'd been drinking from the water bottles of liquor they'd found.

"No. Those must be from some other time."

Then, I was left alone in the car for awhile as they continued their search, taking objects as they saw fit. I watched Ferris crying his eyes out in the other car and wanted to get his attention and make some sort of hopeless effort to cheer him up, but in a brief moment of clarity I decided that tapping on the window with my foot might be seen as some sort of escape attempt. After who knows how long, the cop car with Ferris in it and Ferris's car were both driven off. The remaining cop relocated us to an empty parking lot nearby. He told me he was going to write out a possession ticket, uncuff me, give me my things back, and send me on my way.

As he wrote the ticket, I asked, "Can I talk?"

"Yeah, what'd you wanna know?"

"What happened to my sister?"

"We sent her home."

"Did she get in any trouble?"

"No."

"Good...What happened with my friend?"

He explained that Ferris was getting a DUI, spending the night in jail, and how since it was his second offense he was looking at mandatory jail time.

"Does he need to be bailed out?"

"No, a responsible adult, not you or your sister, has to get him in the morning."

The cop explained what to do to pay the ticket, got me out of the car, took the cuffs off, and gave me my stuff along with the ticket. Then, he offered me a ride home. I didn't take him up on that, but it's kinda odd that my sister was forced to walk home after they had confiscated her mace yet they offered me a ride home, but who am I to question the methods of the police. All that said, adding the association of car rides with getting busted to their association with imminent death has done wonders for my paranoia.

As we pull into the circular drive that goes around the university's main building we see the anorexic girl who has been perpetually running laps around the road for years. On our way past her we barely graze her with the mirror of the car and she crumples to the ground only to pop up a second later and continue on like one of those red skeletons from a <u>Castlevania</u> game.

I look at my dad to make sure I was just imagining that and he pulls over in front of one of the entrances as if nothing had happened.

I guess I'll just have to trust that he would've noticed if that had really happened.

He tells me, "I'll see you in a couple hours."

As I get out of the car I say, "I'll seeya then." and close the door behind me.

Chapter 5

Cigarettes and Silence

I make my way into the building, through the music/art department, and out the other side. A couple quick right turns, up a small set of concrete stairs, and another turn right gets me to where I'm headed.

Most smokers, at least those of us that know about it, call this "the warm spot." It's a must when smoking on cold winter days to be kept warm by the art department's chemical exhaust. My friend Charlie, if I can still call him a friend, is already sitting there on the concrete blocks that form a sorta sit-in ashtray around the vent.

A year ago there would've been five or six people I know chilling out here and bullshitin', but almost all of them stopped going to college here for a variety reasons. Ferris failed too many classes because he was busy drinking, tired of his math major, and too busy fucking and stealing away Tracy from Charlie—who she was engaged to and in a six or more year relationship with. Now Ferris goes to the local technical college. Tracy, on the other hand, was too busy juggling cheating on her boyfriend with a plethora of guys to put much effort

toward school. I suppose I'll get into the details of that
love triangle momentarily though. There was Mary, who
no matter how hard both Ferris and I try to shake it off we
are both to some degree very much in love with. She was
struggling too much financially as she tried to get out on
her own feet to put much effort towards the schooling that
she can't afford right now. Aside from Charlie and myself,
our friend Glenn is the only other member of what once
was our group that still goes here, but as usual his classes
are later in the day.

I say, "Hey," as I join Charlie.
"Hey," he responds, giving me a look that says, 'I hate
you, you fucking scum fucking traitor.'
"How's it goin'?"
"Eh, alright."
"So..." I pause to light a cigarette, "What have you
been up to?"
"Eh, not much, work... school."
Well, you can't say I didn't at least try to make some
sorta conversation, but it's kinda hard to carry a
conversation on your own, especially when the other
person doesn't wanna talk to you at all.

Charlie hates us all now since no one told him about
Tracy cheating on him. I don't think it ever really was our
place to tell him and I told both Tracy and Ferris that they
should tell him themselves, but they put it off over and
over again until he found out by other means. He
took/takes that as everyone betraying him and choosing
Tracy over him, a gross over-simplification. These days I
hear from Tracy, who still talks to him but is an incredibly

unreliable source, that he's become very emo. I guess all he does is hang out at IHOP and play kick-ball with a bunch of kids that are still in high school.

Supposedly, Charlie is happy to have them as his friends—as they are "much better friends than we ever were," since they "don't only care about getting fucked up." I assume that instead of getting fucked up they are busy wallowing in their own depression, having contests to see who can look the most androgynous, and doing a great deal of self-mutilation. At least we were trying to do something about our problems, futile and foolish as it was to try and escape them, but intoxication did allow us to succeed—even if only temporarily.

"How are your classes?" I ask, making another attempt at small talk.

"Not too bad."

He doesn't ask, but I answer the question as well anyways, "I have a twelve hour day on Tuesdays which sucks, but that makes it so I only have a couple days of school a week."

"Damn," he says, stroking his beard with disinterest.

I've know Charlie for 6 or 7 years now. I first met him way back when I started smoking pot regularly and hanging out with the earliest incarnation of our group of friends. At the time he was dating one of the most disgusting creatures in the world. Most people unaffectionately referred to her as "Scabs" on account of her legs, which she showed off way too often and with way too much pride, being covered with scabs. Shortly after we started hanging out, he met Tracy when her former asshole of a boyfriend told him, "I know this girl, Tracy. She wants to fuck you." and in about a week, after a couple dates, Charlie left "Scabs" for her.

Tracy and I had already known each other through mutual friends at school, but we didn't get to know each other very well until after the two of them started dating. Over the years, Tracy and my relationship grew to have a sort of psychiatrist-patient dynamic, since she often confided in me about her problems and I'd give her my best and honest advice—though it was rarely, if ever, taken. Charlie and I on the other hand were never much more than pot smoking buddies, and even that relationship decayed into one of distrust and jealousy on his part.

I look up at Charlie and start to open my mouth to say something, but when he glances over at me I am at a loss for words, so I just awkwardly look down at the ground near my feet.

There are a couple of reasons why Charlie never really trusted me. We got along well enough, but I'm pretty sure he started to really dislike me not long after he and Tracy started seeing each other. I can only really blame myself though, because I can pin point the moment that his opinion of me shifted. It was at Glenn's ex-girlfriend's high school graduation party.

I was wasted as shit and had done a lot of stupid things throughout the day having drunk over half of a 1.75 liter bottle of Jay Bavey, so I ended up apologizing to everyone that happened to be in the room individually. When I got to Charlie I wanted to apologize for accidentally getting a glimpse of Tracy's monstrous bush while she pissed in the doorless closet-like bathroom that was in the back corner of the bedroom. What came out though, was an assholish reference to how he didn't have sex with her in the other bedroom, despite the fact that she had drunkenly begged for it.

"I'm sowry, Chawrie!" I slurred.

Raising an eyebrow he asked, "Why?"

The mischievous look on my face had everyone waiting for an entertaining statement. "Because.... if fie wuzzes drunkes I was now... I'da taken Tracy in da udder room.... an fucked 'er!"

Everyone laughed. Shit, Charlie even laughed reluctantly, but even though he pretended to take it as drunken belligerence I know he has always held that comment against me.

I light another cigarette and Charlie follows suit pulling a smoke out of his pack. When he goes to light it he is only able to get sparks out of his lighter. He holds the lighter up to his ear and shakes it a bit listening for any remaining fluid. After trying a few more tries he looks over at me, but refrains from asking for a light.

When Charlie starts to look through his pockets I pull out my lighter and hold it out to him asking, "Need a light?"

He shakes his head and says, "No I got it." as he continues to dig through his pockets.

"Alllriiight." I say hesitantly, as I slowly start to put the lighter away.

Coming up empty on one last ditch effort to pull a working lighter out like some sorta magic trick, Charlie holds out a hand saying, "Actually, if you don't mind..."

I hand him the lighter saying, "Here ya go."

Charlie lights his cigarette and hands it back to me while choking out a, "Thank you."

"No problem."

Another happening that put fear in him and added to his jealousy of my friendship with Tracy was the inappropriate relationship I had with Helen, our friend Neil's ex-girlfreind. That probably sounds bad, but in my defense it was innocent for the most part, and she initiated it telling me about her interest in me or at least by implying she was interested in me by asking if I ever thought of her as more than a friend. I answered honestly and she told me that she was interested in me as well. She was my first kiss, but in all reality she just used me to make Neil jealous.

Charlie held that occurrence against me more than Neil ever did, fearing that I'd steal Tracy away from him. Though admittedly I'd commit this infraction again with Mary, I cut short all of Tracy's efforts to make Charlie's fear actualized. At one point she even temporarily broke up with Charlie and asked me to take her to winter formal, but I was determined to do what I thought was morally right at the time, mainly since I didn't think I'd be able to get away without any trouble and I knew whether it was best for her or not she would just end up running back to Charlie as she always did.

We got together one day for lunch and talked, but I made it clear that nothing could happen between the two of us until her and Charlie were done and he was either over her or had ended up with someone else. Avoiding the temptation was made much easier though, thanks to David

Bowie since the image of him from <u>Labyrinth</u> stared at me from her chest the whole time we talked. Shortly after we had that conversation, she and Charlie got back together and though it was never brought up, I know this solidified me in his mind as a villain.

Charlie and I continue to sit in relative silence. He shoots me the occasional scowl and I find myself somehow managing to shrug without moving a muscle.

You know, normally I don't mind awkward moments all that much. I tend to dwell in the realm of the awkward. Everything feels kinda awkward to me, I generally feel out of place regardless of where I am, or who I'm with. The two of us sitting here right now though... this is... well, it bothers even me. The amount of common ground we had has shrunk over the years as he stopped smoking weed and doing any drugs quite some time ago, and it has been years since they days that we used to play <u>Perfect Dark</u> together on a daily basis. Now we would have little to talk about even if it wasn't for what happened between Ferris and Tracy.

I have always wondered what came first, Charlie's jealousy and lack of trust or Tracy cheating on him, but cyclically both escalated throughout their relationship. He wanted to control how she dressed, among other things, in order to prevent her from cheating on him. Meanwhile, she cheated on him out of anger and defiance. Granted I'm over-simplifying as well, but that is one of the major issues of their failed relationship and it has been left unexamined during the course of their many breakups. Instead, the blame has been tossed around—always landing where it doesn't belong. Tracy was always looking for a way out, but was unwilling to be alone and eventually she ended up finding that way out, with Ferris.

"So..." I pause for a moment to reconsider the thought that I was about to blurt out.

Charlie looks at me as I fumble around to light another cigarette.

Shouldn't I be apologizing?

Why? You don't feel bad about it.

...

Well, maybe a little, but only about how it all went down. That was out of your control though.

I speak up saying, "So, I guess after all this time Ferris was the one you really needed to watch out for."

Charlie half smirks as he pulls out a cigarette of his own. I hold out my lighter and he takes it saying, "Yeah, I guess." before lighting his smoke. He tosses the lighter back to me with just enough extra force to make it an unfriendly gesture. He asks, "When did you find out about the two of them?"

"Hmm..." I stall taking I few hits off my cigarette, "...I'm not sure exactly when, but it was probably a couple weeks after my sister's birthday. Tracy and I went out for drinks and she was being all dramatic, talking about how she'd broken up with you and wasn't sure if the guy she was interested in was going to choose her over his girlfriend."

Charlie corrects me saying, "Actually, she hadn't broken up with me yet."

"Really?"

"Yeah."

"Well, regardless, as far as she was concerned the two of you were over and done with." I pause as Charlie grumbles to himself for a moment before I continue on, "Anyhow, I guessed that it was Ferris since I had my suspicions when she would only let him take care of her drunk ass on my sis's birthday and based off her awkward reaction I knew I was right. I didn't know for sure though, till later that night when after a lot of prodding and poking she admitted it to me."

I leave out the fact that she didn't want to tell me, because she thought "it would hurt me" so to get her to finally admit it to me, it took putting a handful of cigarettes out in the palm of my hand to illustrate the fact that what hurt me was the frustration that all the lying and bullshit gave me, not any sense of jealousy or feeling of inferiority to Ferris. The feeling of inferiority was there, but not because of her. It was there because he'd always succeeded where I had so often failed and he was loved by so many women while none loved me. The only way in which I was even remotely jealous of his relationship with Tracy was that he had taken away the emotional dependence on me that she had developed over the years. I was no longer needed, and being needed is the closest thing to love that I've experienced. Tracy always tells me that I'm like her best friend. I have come to realize though, that this is only when it's convenient for her, and she wants a shoulder to cry on, or someone willing to listen to her bullshit problems. As much as I stretch my mind I can't remember a single fucking thing she has ever done for me.

"I guess they ended up having sex on the beach that night." I add.

"Yea, so I heard," he says, "apparently they slept together a few times while she and I were still together."

"When did that all start?" I ask.

"He fucking kissed her on New Year's Eve... in my fucking house!"

"Shit, when did that happen? I was there."

"Eh, you were probably too busy fawning over Mary."

Shrugging, I admit, "I do tend to do that."

After a moment of silence, he asks me, "Why didn't you? ... Why didn't anyone tell me?"

"I can only speak for myself... but I never felt like it was my place. I told them they needed to talk to you about it and they kept saying they would, but obviously..."

"Yea, I had to end up hearing it from Glenn and Nina."

"How's the tooth by the way?" I ask.

After being told about everything by Glenn and his sister Nina, who was or is, (it's hard to keep track), supposedly Tracy's best friend, Charlie repeatedly thanked Glenn and told him he was a "great guy." This praise, however, angered Glenn who was drunk as fuck and feeling very guilty about not telling Charlie much sooner—so his instinctual response was to tell Charlie to "fuck off" and punch him in the face, chipping his tooth.

Feeling the tooth in his mouth Charlie says, "Eh, alright, the dentist did a pretty good job."

"I guess you should never tell Glenn he's a good guy."

He lets out a singular laugh and says, "Yeah."

After being punched, Charlie texted what he had learned from Glenn and Nina to both Tracy and Ferris's now ex-girlfriend, who Charlie had been hoping to hook up with wanting some sort of temporary girlfriend exchange even before he and Tracy had broken up.

When our usual bar emptied out that night, Ferris's ex attacked Tracy in the parking and sent her reeling with a strong sucker-punch before anyone could do anything to stop it. Chaos burst out in the parking lot.

Accusations of who had given each other "HPB," flew around in all directions.

Tracy waved a poor excuse for a knife around as she screeched out obscenities.

An overweight semi-retarded hipster started attacking someone who was trying to hold one of the girls back. He repeatedly yelled out, "You don't hit girls." and as he did this he picked up a girl who was in his way, and threw her to the ground.

(I suppose that doesn't constitute "hitting", so make note of it if you're a potentially abusive or just plain abusive spouse.)

Random guys kept rushing over drunkenly looking for a fight and asking, "Who's hittin' girls!?!"

I got some very confused looks as I told them all, "Apparently everyone!"

The cops were called, and everyone skulked away. The wild hipster accused Tracy of stabbing him, "Five times!" he emphasized—yet he was among the first people to flee the scene.

My sister and I got into a friend's car and left to go smoke a bowl. After we pulled away, she handed me the knife that Tracy had been waving around.

Charlie and I both pull out another smoke, I light mine and hand him the lighter.

As he lights his cigarette I ask, "Did you go to the bar that night?"

He returns the lighter while answering, "No, I heard about it though. Tracy stabbing some guy and whatnot."

"Yea, I'm still on the fence about that, at the very least though the word stabbing isn't very accurate. He only had some shallow cuts in his arm."

"Yea..."

No one can be completely sure if Tracy actually stabbed that idiot, or they aren't about to admit it. Any noncircumstantial evidence was lost when I threw that shitty little wannabe-Nazi boot knife into the lake. He was known to cut himself for a wide variety of reasons so the wounds could have been self-inflicted, but despite the fact that during a couple of Tracy's crying fits I agreed when she said, "You know me, I'm not capable of something like that." in all honesty I think she slashed him very poorly a few times rather than actually "stabbing" him.

I know her!

And yes she would do something like that, she was angry and drunk and not in control of herself, it's a miracle she didn't hurt anyone that was trying to help her. The fucking hypocrite deserved much worse than what he got though.

I look at my watch muttering, "Shit, gotta get to class."

Charlie looks at his watch as I stand up, grab my bag, and power through the remainder of my cigarette.

"I better get goin' too." he says.

We both flick are cigarette butts into the dirt and walk inside then head separate ways with a simultaneous obligatory, "Cya."

I wonder if I will ever see him again. He'll probably avoid the "warm spot" around this time from now on. This was a pretty damn rare occurrence as it's been a few months since I last saw him. You know, he is quick to play the victim, but shortly after he found out about Ferris and Tracy—Charlie proved he was just a petty and spiteful person who only wanted someone to see him as good, even if he'd never felt anything but disgust for them.

In an attempt to prove he was not a hypocrite, he told one of our other friend's girlfriends, now ex-girlfriend as a result, about how she had been cheated on. Now, in her eyes Charlie is a great guy; she even wanted to hook up with him and told him that when she loses weight and is super hot he'll want her. On the other hand the rest of us are all, "...piece of shit fucking liars!"

Well maybe we are, but I've never really believed in the concept of lies of omission. That's just not saying something. Hell, I could call the truth a lie of truthfulness in the same spirit.

I'm an honest person, even if it turns out I have no other redeeming qualities, that's why I keep my mouth shut a lot; my honesty is far too brutal for most. Also, the fact that I know about her trying to hook up with Charlie should make her examine the integrity of the people who she currently calls friends.

But here I am, the always dreaded classroom door...

Chapter 6

The Cure for Classroom Narcolepsy

Walking into the classroom, I scan around for empty seats.

One of the few perks of the assigned seating we always had up through high school was at least you always knew you'd have a place to sit. It was luck of the draw—though mostly based on how much the teacher liked you—but whether you were next to the hottest girl in the class, the annoying know it all, the kid whose voice made you wonder if he had down syndrome, or the bastard who smelt like he used dog shit for soap—at least you knew for sure that you'd have a place to sit. Take that away, and unless you show up to class 10 to 15 minutes early you're gonna have to stand there feeling like a total idiot as you try to find the closest desk not obstructed by a barricade of airport luggage. It never gets easier either; every time you stand there assaulted by the eyes of your classmates feeling just as stupid as the first time.

There's the one!

On the other side of the room: near a door, one row over, and two seats from the front. Doesn't look like anyone has laid claim to it yet.

The teacher organizes her books and notes for the class as I make my way to that desk. I have to step over one after another of those damn wheeled luggage cases, but I make it to my seat and sit down without bringing too much attention to myself.

What the fuck is the deal with these people?

You shouldn't need a bag for school that wouldn't even qualify as a carry-on. I don't care how many fucking classes you're taking; you shouldn't need that much shit.

And it doesn't help that all the fucking hallways have brick floors.

When you try to take a nap in between classes it sounds like you're in the 19th century, hearing a parade of horse drawn carriages go by.

Are people so weak that they can't carry their books in some sort of briefcase, or god forbid a traditional backpack?

Half of these bastards can't even pick the damn things up to traverse a small flight of stairs. They'll take an elevator or use the wheel chair ramp. On a rare occasion you might see someone roll it up the stairs, step by fucking step, but you're more likely to see someone in a wheel chair make an attempt than you are to see these lazy cock suckers do it. I can excuse the elderly and even to a certain extent the obese, but when I see someone who is obviously in much better shape than me I just wanna beat them to death with their own fucking luggage.

Anyhow, I pull my notebook and the oversized, overpriced book for the class out of my bag then put them on my desk. As the teacher takes roll, which I'm lucky enough to always be near the beginning of, I scan the room for the best looking and most scantily clad girls in the class. I always like to know who I can check out periodically throughout the course of the lecture, and I try to learn their names from the roll call for the purpose of adding an element of realism to future masturbatory fantasies.

Holy cleavage!

It's a shame I missed the name that goes with those knockers.

And what was it?

Kate?

I've had classes with her before.

She's not the type that would stick out in a crowd, but she's cute—and that skirt, those thighs, and the way that she crosses and uncrosses her legs makes me strain my neck for the right angle to get a glimpse of panties, or lack thereof—but there's never quite the right lighting.

But those smooth thighs... I want them wrapped around me.

Down boy, down.

That's not appropriate in public, and people often say it's even illegal.

Since when were there notes on the board.

I quickly scribble them down and try not to drift off into sleep, or some sort of sex fantasy, as the teacher drones on. The classroom is not the place for a wet dream complete with the moaning of someone-I've-never-even-been-properly-introduced-to's name.

Before the professor starts droning on about some crap I have no intention of paying attention to, I nod off for a second leaving a streak of ink across the page of my notebook. Barely waking up in time to catch myself from falling out of my desk, I sit up straight. My eyes are drawn to Kate's thighs as if they were magnetized. Her legs cross, uncross, and re-cross—like some sorta sexual metronome, and I throb to their beat.

I feel it's necessary to pause here for a moment in order to state two things. The first being, that Kate is sitting practically next to me on my left, but slightly behind me due to the un-uniform arrangement of the desks. This gives me the perfect, non-obvious view of those bare legs of hers as well as a decent position to catch a glimpse of her small, but well proportioned and perky bosom—which shows exquisitely in her semi-low-cut top. The second is, yes, I am something of a pervert, but it can't really be helped—she's right there, and being a 22 year old virgin, who has never even had a girlfriend and has only kissed two girls in his entire life—I am an incredibly horny and sexually frustrated individual.

Anyway, I've hated school for as long as I can remember.

The third grade is the starting point of these memories. I had entered what they called "the enrichment program." Challenging the smarter kids so they don't get bored and teaching them at an accelerated rate isn't a bad idea in theory; however, few of us ever felt truly challenged and we were all just as bored by it as we were by regular classes. Also, in practice it is a horrible thing to do to kids, as it completely undermines the socialization process that is the most important part of our education system, especially when it comes to elementary school.

It separated us "smarter" kids from everyone else, and this had a few incredibly bad side effects. It gave us an unhealthy sense of superiority to our peers, alienating us from the rest of the kids in the school. Jealousy and a sense of opposition grew in the "normal" kids, forming an insurmountable divide within the school. This most obviously manifested itself by the "normal" kids picking on and bullying the "gifted" ones treating them as if "gifted" really meant retarded. By alienating us from the majority of our peers that important socialization process was severely hindered. On top of that, while every year the "normal" kids were forced to meet and interact with new people we just formed a tight knit group that was in the same class for four years straight. Then, we were broken apart and spread out across the city to go to different junior high schools.

Legs gracefully uncross and switch positions, her left leg now draped over the right.

I don't know what it is about the way her thighs press against each other that fascinates and arouses me. Maybe it's what's in between them that really interests me. Not necessarily her pussy, but the space between her legs— that void sucks me in. Sorta like cleavage, it's not the breasts themselves that are the most fascinating, not that they aren't fascinating in their own right, there's something known as side boob that's just as fascinating as cleavage, but it's the way the tits press against each other and the space in between them that really pulls your gaze in. Maybe it's just the subtle motion of her crossing legs that attracts my attention. Most likely, it's a combination of many factors including the fact that the way her legs press against each other and intertwine it's almost as if they are two lovers shifting positions, but never ceasing to rub their bodies against each other.

Elementary school in reality wasn't all that bad, but I only grew to hate school more as I went on to junior high. Only a couple of my friends from elementary went to the same junior high that I did. My best friend did, but his mom made him not take the honors classes, he quickly made new friends, and in a matter of months we stopped talking altogether. I didn't make any real friends there, only the need-someone-to-sit-at-lunch-and-do-group-work-with type of friends. I wasn't cool enough for the luxury of friends. Most of the people thought I was some sort of Satanist, or perverted rapist, and were afraid of me with no real justification.

Perverted, I'll give 'em that, but rapist, no. I'm sure most of them would be much more likely to rape a person than me; some might've even forced their will on an animal or two by now. The only good part was that it was a block away from my house, and I was happy as hell that they changed to the middle school system so I only had to spend two years there.

High
   school...

High   ...\ /...   school...

         school
   High...

Sorry, almost got a glimpse of panties and nearly had one of those anime style nosebleed moments.

Anyway, high school was better than junior high, but that's not saying much. I went to a new and supposedly more technologically advanced school. It divided itself into three departments: business, which was composed mostly of your typical preppy future frat boy and date rape victim crowd; biotechnology, which had that same crowd along with a good portion of the goth, punk, and emo kids who mainly were interested in science since it could lead them to seeing corpses, they hoped for mutilated ones; and communications, which was just a mix of every type of kid you can think of, but social outcasts were the majority.

It's strange that I was in the communications department given my lack of communication skills, but it was supposed to be more about film and computers than anything else. Making movies was my passion at the time; in my spare time I'd written quite a few admittedly horrible, but still interesting screenplays. I wanted to make films with my brother and our group of like-minded friends, however, the schools film department was a huge disappointment as it was composed of a few shoddy video cameras, a studio taken straight from the 80s, a few IMacs for editing, and a total of three or four classes at most. Instead of preparing me for further film related schooling it killed my passion for movies for quite some time.

I had already lost faith in being taught anything worth knowing, which made paying attention or even giving anything a chance virtually impossible. I was a good student though: one of the smartest kids in class, didn't talk much either to distract everyone or to try and make

the teacher seem stupid, didn't goof off, got good grades, I
was witty when I needed to be, and I would help the other
kids—but only if they asked.

That allowed me the one luxury I wanted: the ability to
sleep in and often through the entirety of every class,
seldom getting in any trouble for it. Occasionally, I'd
frustrate a teacher or two since they didn't like seeing one
of the few kids worth bothering with not give a damn.
That sleep during school though, was instrumental when it
came to keeping up with late nights of drinking, pot
smoking, and drug experimentation. Sometimes, I'd wake
up in class still fucked up, and wonder how the fuck I even
got there.

While my antics in between classes were hardly those
of a good student, there were only a few occasions that I
got in any trouble. I got caught the one time I had a
cigarette outside after school, but due to the fact that I
looked like I'd been living on the streets for years with my
scraggly full beard, messy hair, and the layers of coats I
was wearing—I had more trouble convincing them that I
was actually a student than anything else.

One time I dedicated a period of study hall to
meditating rather than sleeping and I was accused of and
interrogated about being on drugs, but after multiple
phone calls to my parents I ended up getting out of school
early that day and was told to have something to eat in the
morning to go with the Paxil I was prescribed to take at
the time.

The graphic design teacher and the school counselor
didn't appreciate the artistic value of my self-defining
logo being a time bomb that was about to go off, but
despite the fact that they were convinced I was gonna

attempt to blow the school up I never got in any real trouble; I was just inconvenienced by their false concern for my well being.

God damn those thighs are distracting!
So smooth and...
                                        ...ripe.
I couldn't pay attention to the lecture if I wanted to.

I suppose that brings me to college.

Definitely the best educational institution I've had for the most part the opposite of pleasure to be a part of. I wouldn't even be here if it wasn't for the fact that my mom and grandma consider it a mandatory part of my education. The main reason it isn't actually mandatory is probably because if it was, the universities couldn't charge people an arm and a leg and the resulting astronomical rise in taxes wouldn't go over too well.

But I can smoke outside without worrying, which I couldn't even do once I'd turned 18 in high school, and I suppose I've learned a few things worth learning, though mainly I've just been introduced to new perspectives that life would've given me eventually anyways. There's a better quality of teachers, or rather professors, and I've had a few really cool classes but the majority of it hasn't been all that different from high school. Everyone still has their same cliques, the same preconceived ideas about anyone that's not a part of theirs, and we're all still spoon fed a shit load of worthless knowledge.

There is one great thing about it however.

The great amount of thigh cand... I mean eye candy. There's that pre-winter boob parade and the daily spring boob parades as well as a good amount of hot girls in general regardless of: how much bare skin they're showing, how well formed their cleavage is, or how their thighs rub against each other.

I have always found it strange that for some reason, despite my hate of school in all its forms, I've always excelled at it. I'm not even all that smart when it really comes down to it; I know plenty of people that I'm sure have lower IQs than me who know a lot more than I do—whether it be about a specific subject, or just general knowledge regardless of the subject matter. What I really excel at is transferring knowledge from one piece of paper to another one, and that is why I'm practically a genius on paper. You could ask me about: something I just aced a test on, something that was in one of my favorite books, a movie I've seen a hundred times, a video game I've played for hours, or even this very book you're reading—and chances are you'd get a blank stare and nine out of ten times even if my synapses started firing and I was able to formulate any coherent thoughts they would build up like phlegm in my throat and come out in disgusting indecipherable globs. Only with a great deal of time and some paper or a keyboard will I be able to translate those thoughts for you.

Now why is everyone standing up?

Shit, class is over. I didn't even look at my watch. Usually that's all I really pay any significant amount of attention to.

Thank you Kate, your incredible thighs made this horribly boring class enjoyable for once. Wear a skirt more often, please, and you might want to even consider something an inch or two shorter.

As I gather my things I try to communicate that to her telepathically.

Chapter 7

Home is Where the Food is

I put my notebook of scribbling and the unopened textbook away, taking care to spend enough time getting my shit together for Kate to be the person that leaves the room directly before me.

I suppose it probably sounds stalkeresque, but I doubt there's anyone out there who hasn't positioned themselves near a person that they had the hots for, at least once, and it's not as if I'm going out of my way to follow that sweet ass. I'm just enjoying the view till our paths no longer coincide.

There
she
goes.

As Kate leaves my line of sight I pull a cigarette out of the pack in my shirt pocket and put it in my mouth then grab my lighter, increase speed, and twirl it around between my fingers heading towards the school's main entrance. I weave my way through the crowded hall with the reckless precision of a drunk on ether: constantly on the verge of bumping into someone, but never quite making contact. Those watching me stumble around in this fashion would probably think I was doing an impression of Johnny Depp playing Jack Sparrow, but this is just how I've always tended to get around. In no time at all I get outside, light the cigarette, take a seat on one of the short concrete walls near the road, and look to see if my dad is pulling up yet.

Good, I got time to finish this smoke.

I watch the parking lot shuttle bus pull up and Glenn gets off of it carrying the massive amount of crap he needs for the art classes he's taking in order to get a Web Design certificate, or whatever the fuck they call it.

He comes over to me saying, "Hey!"

"Hey man."

He recklessly throws all the crap he's carrying to the ground and lights up a cigarette.

I ask, "How's it going, man?"

"Alright, be better if I didn't have to carry all this shit around though."

"Yea, that's what you get for taking art classes."

"It sucks, but I have to take 'em."

I nod as I flick my cigarette into the street and light another one since I don't see my dad pulling up.

Glenn asks, "So, anything new and exciting?"

"Not really, I've just been doing the school thing, writing, and playing a lot of Battlefield 2142."

"I figured that, I saw your stats, fuckin' ridiculous."

"Yea, since I got it, if I'm at home I'm usually playing it. I'm startin' to get burnt out on it though."

"Yea... You know about the transport exploit in Titan mode?"

"No, what's that?"

"You get a couple of people in the transport chopper and just hover over the enemy titan and switch seats; everyone gets a shit load of points for it."

"That's fucked up."

"Have you been in any games where people had scores in the thousands?"

"Yea."

"They're doin' that."

"Shit, I thought they were just really good at getting resupply points."

"Nah, they're using that trick, but if you see peoples' scores going up like that you can just get on the guns, blast the shit out of 'em, and get a crap-load of points and pins."

"Nice."

Glenn flicks his cigarette into the street and looks at his cellphone. "Well, gotta get to class." He picks up all his shit and adds, "You wanna hang out later?"

"Yea, it's been awhile."

"Yea, I'll probably get on AIM after class, if not I'll call ya."

"Okay, cool, I'll seeya later man."

"Seeya."

He heads into the building. After a couple of minutes of smoking and spacing out, my dad pulls up just as I finish the cigarette. I pick up my bag and get in the car.

"Hi Alden."

"Hey."

"How was school?"

You know the answer's never gonna change, but I admire your persistence in always asking it.

"Uhh...it was ... school."

I sniff the air to try and tell if he's been drinking. Paranoia says he has, but to me the car always has a slight hint of that whiskey smell in it for some reason. I space out for the majority of the car ride and we make it back to the house without incident. People who drive often tell me that at times they arrive at their destination with no memory of the drive itself. I tell them this happens much more frequently to passengers, which is why we are so horrible at giving directions.

My dad parks in front of the house and I get out of the car. I make my way to the front door where I start fumbling with my keys.

Keys in hand, my dad says, "I got it Alden."

I stop fumbling around and let him unlock and open the door. We are immediately greeted by our almost morbidly, but regardlessly obese beagle who excitedly shuffles in from the living room barely able to carry its own weight. I pet the dog, put my bag on the table, drape my jacket over my chair, light my back-at-home cigarette, and start rummaging through the fridge.

What to eat?

What to eat?

Let's see.

Eggs?

Save that for a back up.

Quesadilla?

No! Microwaved cheese between two tortillas just isn't that appealing after the thousandth time.

What else?

Bread?

Bah!

Cottage cheese?
That's even more flavorless than a quesadilla.
Grilled cheese maybe?
Nope, don't have those individually wrapped cheese squares.

Why is it that those crappy things always taste good in grilled cheese while other cheese doesn't? It's barely even real cheese, but put it between two pieces of bread buttered on the outside, fry it up or put it in one of those flip-top sandwich-o-matics, and bam you got something delicious. Maybe it's the act of burning the butter into the bread. Things just seem to taste better the closer they get to clogging an artery, but that still doesn't explain why better quality cheese doesn't taste as good in a grilled cheese sandwich. Solving that mystery won't make me any less hungry though.

Well, it looks like the fridge is out, aside from a last resort omelet.
What's in the freezer?
Let's see, brats and bacon. I'll put those in the fridge to thaw. At least I know I'll have something good to eat tomorrow.
Frozen pizza?
Any with meat on 'em?
Let's see:
veggie supreme,
                veggie supreme,
        extra cheese,
                        extra cheese,
                            three cheese,

four cheese,

and...

supreme...

nope, fucking veggie supreme again.

Damn it, why do we force the vegetarian to do the grocery shopping?

And why the fuck is there never any real difference between extra cheese, three cheese, and four cheese? The extra cheese especially pisses me off. If a company doesn't even have a cheese pizza among their products how can they say these pizzas have extra cheese? By the look of 'em they probably mean that they just used the extra cheese leftover after all the other pizzas were made.

Hmm, fries?

No good on their own.

Various Budget Gourmet side dishes?

I'll resort to eggs before that.

And what the hell is that?

Don't know, and I don't really wanna know. Whatever it is it's been in the back there far too long to still be edible.

Why not throw it away?

Well... it makes the freezer seem less empty I guess.

I close the freezer and kick around the cigarette ash that accumulated on the floor during my search. I ash the little bit that didn't make it to the floor in the ashtray.

"Find anything?" my dad asks.

"Yeah, but nothin' I feel like eating."

Maybe there's something in the pantry.

Damn it, none of those meal in a box things.

Looks like it's down to ramen, rice, or pasta—and not even the flavored Pasta-Roni type shit.

I don't really feel like washing out and firing up the rice cooker, especially when there isn't any thawed meat to have on the side.

It looks like it's gonna be eggs.

I give the fridge and freezer another once over.

Didn't miss anything.

Just eggs is hardly a meal.

Hmm.

I finish the cigarette, going over the inventory of the fridge, freezer, and pantry in my head.

...

...

I know.

Ramelet!

I grab two packs of ramen out of the pantry, put the ramen into a pot along with the flavoring, and fill the pot with enough water to submerge the ramen. I put that on the stove to boil then grab the eggs and butter out of the fridge and set them on the counter. I grab a fork and a large pan then scoop a massive chunk of butter into it. Once that's for the most part melted I crack five eggs into the pan, lower the heat, throw the shells away, wash my hands, and put the rest of the eggs and butter back in the fridge. I chop up some chives and take some canned tomatoes and peppers then mix all that in with the eggs. Once it starts to boil, I drain the ramen in the sink and stir around the omelet allowing it to cook a little more. Once the eggs reach the right consistency, not quite cooked all the way but not extremely runny, I add the ramen to the pan. I mix it all together so the ramen is coated in egg and fry it up for a couple minutes.

Voila, ramelet!

I turn the burner off and put the ramelet onto a plate then excessively add salt and pepper. I stab my fork into the ramelet and set the plate on the counter before looking down at my pack of cigarettes.

Almost out.

Grabbing my jacket and putting it on, I announce, "Gotta get smokes." then make my way out the door and across the street to the store.

Out in front of the corner store a bunch of punk ass kids are sitting there waiting for their turn to get inside and try to steal some candy while the Koreans that currently run the place aren't looking. I step over one of their bikes and go inside. The two kids that have been allowed in are at the counter counting out nickels and dimes to pay for their candy. They put some back as they argue about who gets what while pocketing more than they pay for. Once they're finally done I approach the counter.

"Cigewets?" the clerk asks.

"Yea."

I give him a five and he sets a soft pack of Marlboro Reds on the counter then gives me my change from the pile of dimes and nickels that the middle-schoolers paid with. I pocket the change, grab my smokes, and say, "Have a nice day."

He says, "Zyou too," as I make my way out the door passing a couple more punk kids that wanna try their luck at shoplifting.

It's weird that they obey the two students inside at a time rule, but they don't follow any others. Nearly every time I see kids in there one of 'em gets caught stealing. Not to mention the fact that the cops are called on these little fuckers on almost a weekly basis, because 40 to 60 of them will have a brawl in the middle of the street worthy of a modern action movie where numbers are more important than good fight choreography.

I go back into the house, grab the ramelet, my bag, and my soda then head downstairs into my room.

Chapter 8

Bored Enough to Kill God

In the basement, I'm greeted by the incessant meows of our two cats, who both want more food.

"Wait just a goddamn minute you bastards."

I put my bag in its usual spot on the floor, set my plate down, crack open my soda, and take a quick swig before setting it down on the table.

While grabbing the cup next to the cat food, I say, "Alright you bastards, I'll give you your food." I quickly scoop up their food and pour it into the empty dish on the floor. As soon as the food hits the dish, they stop meowing.

I hurry back over to my own food telling them, "There! Now leave me the fuck alone!"

I take off my jacket and toss it onto the futon then sit in my chair, switch my computer monitor/TV to TV mode, and start to chow into my ramelet.

I hope I won't have to change the channel from Comedy Central, because some horrible movie like Zoolander is playing for the hundredth time this week.

At least the crappy 80s movies they used to repeatedly show we're halfway decent, but when it's Ben Stiller and

Owen Wilson week, one can't help but reconsider suicide and/or murder.

I let out a sigh of relief as the commercial break ends and Mad TV starts playing.

It's not quite crappy movie hour yet on Comedy Central, and I can handle third rate sketch comedy for the duration of a meal at least. You never know, they've surprised me once or twice and actually made me laugh.

After eating about three fourths of my ramelet I need to take a little break to make room for the rest; I can't refrigerate it to save it for later, because for some reason the process of refrigeration does not bode well for a ramelet. It works fine for ramen and omelets separately, but not as a single entity. You end up with a strangely crusty yet soggy blob of matter that is quite hard to look at, let alone stomach eating.

I light a smoke, set my food aside, and put my feet up.
What to do now?
I pull the computer up on half of the screen.
What to do?
Could play one of many video games I'm in the middle of, but I'm pretty burnt out on most of 'em. Played them way too much, way too quick. Regardless of how fun the new Battlefield is, after nearly 200 hours of gameplay in just a few weeks, I need a break from it—or it'll cease to be any fun at all.

Let's see...
Anime?
What do I have?
There's gotta be something to watch. Afterall, according to the AniDB I've downloaded between 10 and

15 percent of all the anime ever made, or at least that they have catalogued.

Let's see...   Ergo Proxy?

Fuckin' great show, but might as well wait for the last couple episodes to come out to avoid waiting a couple weeks with a complete mind fuck. It's an amazing show to watch while you're tripping. A friend and I watched the first nine on acid after bar close one night, and it was incredible. I wouldn't recommend that to someone new to hallucinogens though, because its insane and dark tone is likely to give a bad trip to an inexperienced user, but the show itself is so philosophically deep and visually amazing that it's like an acid trip in anime form.

Naruto?

Fuck that, I don't know if I'll ever be in the mood to catch up on the crappy filler they've been releasing. It's a great anime, but they've been doing shitty side story episodes for way too long to be tolerable.

Bleach?

Nah, that filler is pretty good, but I'm not really in the mood for catchin' up on a bunch of episodes.

There's a shitload of shows that I'm not even considering since I don't wanna start a new series, most of 'em actually.

I'd watch the last few episodes of Eureka Seven if they'd ever finish downloading.

Hmm...

hentai...

hentai...

hentai...

Damn it, all the short ones are hentais.

Fuck it.

I could look through my CD wallets, but I have the feeling it's just one of those days where nothing seems all that appealing to do.

Wait, was that a new <u>Death Note</u>?

Nope, last week's.

Damn it all.

I put out my cigarette and finish my ramelet then set the plate on a table on the other side of the room.

Looks like there's only one thing to do——pace around my room and argue, or at least converse with myself in my own head. Might be a waste of time, but usually it helps me think up somethin' to do, get some sort of inspiration, or come up with some gem of wisdom.

What'll it be today?

Rehearsal for conversations that will never happen?

Self justifying bullshit?

Or just strange thought experimentation?

I light another cigarette and put my 100 disc changer on random, then start pacing in circles around the basement as The Stones' "Sympathy for the Devil" starts to play.

If there's a god—I'd like to see him show himself before the entire world, give some sort of undeniable proof that he/she/it is god, and explain how despite their differences all of the world's religions are worshiping the same entity.

Wouldn't that be wonderful, and a great step towards peace on Earth?

My version of this delusion, or whatever you'd call it, doesn't end with that sort of heart warming idealism though. Mine ends with a dead god and a world in despair.

Maybe it'd be harder to do if the god turned out to be a beautiful woman, but I've seen enough movies, animes, and TV shows, read enough, and played enough video games to know that evil creatures usually take up the form you're most likely to trust and believe.

Ah, who are you kidding if this god was a woman you'd probly run to the nearest sex shop, and buy her a strap-on so she could bend you over the podium and fuck you like every woman you've ever been interested in.

True, but at least I'd be involved in a sex act for once.

Yea, I suppose it would be better to be literally fucked by one. It'd probably be less painful in the long run, for once you'd actually be relieved when she got bored with you, and then you could shit all over her—and people would still feel sorry for you.

Anyways, once this god makes its speech I want to immediately kill it and watch billions of believers around the world fill up with sorrow and anguish realizing how helpless and pointless their lives really are, and how much time they've wasted trying to earn their way into some sort of great afterlife that can no longer be assured with their god dead.

Now how in the hell do you plan on killing an omnipotent god?

First off, I don't buy into the idea of an omnipotent being. I've had the idea that no matter how good you are there's always someone better engrained into me since childhood and how can anyone, or thing, be all powerful if there's someone or something that's even more all powerful. The phrases more all powerful or more omnipotent seem more ridiculous to me than the idea of a god and creator to begin with.

Even if I could be convinced this god was omnipotent that wouldn't change a thing. If it was omnipotent I'd have to also presume it had that typical godly omnipresence. I'm much more inclined to believe in that concept, having tripped enough to both see and experience the interconnectedness of all things.

If this god is present in me, so is its omnipotence, and therefore its own existence makes me capable of killing it.

Hell, if that's the case, killing myself or anyone else, or even anything else, would be killing god or at least a part of god—even if it's just the equivalent of a dead skin cell.

Wars and genocide must give god dandruff!

Anyhow, if god is present in me it/he/she is partially suicidal and wants me to kill it/she/he. Therefore, I'm confident any attempt to do so would be allowed to succeed. I'd be willing to risk and curious to see the end of all existence as we know it, literal or otherwise.

You're insane!

And you're crazier than me if it took you this long to figure that out, but my insanity doesn't matter, and it definitely doesn't change your inability to even hypothetically defend your god from my wrath right now.

But...

Quiet you, it's too late to save it now.

I wonder what Glenn's ex would think of all that now that she's got a daughter and has found Jesus. I doubt she'd find it all that amusing. I never quite understood why people tend to find God when something good happens in their life. You can deny god and find the idea of him to be ridiculous for years, while hating every moment of your life, but when something good happens it can't just be because probability says it was bound to happen, or that you were lucky, or that your own efforts to better yourself and kick your drug habits made it so your child was able to be born and survive. Instead, you sell yourself short and consider it to be a miracle of god and proof of his existence. Miraculous doesn't necessarily mean there was a god involved.

It seems to me to be an all too common occurrence that someone with an overbearing Christian parent rejects that religion and ends up hating their life, mutilating themselves, and ultimately heavily abusing drugs only to eventually find the religion that they denied when they have a child themselves. That way, they can raise the child to eventually resent them and make the same exact mistakes, or worse ones.

I put out my cigarette and light another one as the CD changer shuffles and loads another disc. It lands on one of my favorite Bob Dylan songs, "Tangled up in Blue."

"You know you're quite an asshole!"
Hey. Ferris?! What are you doing in my ever changing inner monologue? I wasn't even thinkin' about you!
"Well you know I tend to show up in your thoughts when she does."
He gestures towards Mary behind him.

Wait!
I blink a few times to erase these specters of thought from my sight then look at my cigarette to confirm it's just a cigarette and not a joint.

Well, I'm sober.

The thought of Mary is usually the first thing to pop into my head when I hear this song, but it's not often that I actually visualize my thoughts. I'll roll with it though, even if it turns out that I'm finally losing it for real.

Ferris adds, "You've never been a very good host either, but ignoring me. Now you're just being rude."

Oh, you're still here?

"Yes we are, and isn't she hotter than ever?"

Huh?

I turn toward my bed envisioning Mary lying on it. Her perfect, smooth, pale skin shows in all the right places. Her thighs show where black thigh high leggings meet the garter belt that holds them up from under a short red plaid skirt. Her perfect breasts almost pop out of the tight black corset that cinches her waist. Black ribbons hold her fiery red shoulder length hair in pigtails so that her coy smile is unobscured.

My cock throbs as she bats her eyes at me while running a hand along her inner thigh.

Ohhhh... her? Yea, she's definitely hot, that I'll never deny, but hotter than ever... I'm not too sure.

I turn back around, but Ferris has evaporated into a formless voice in my head.

"Come on, why not?"

It's just a different kinda hot; I prefer the old one.

"Why?"

It was more of a natural, sorta innocent kinda hot.

I turn back to the vision of Mary on my bed as she sucks on a finger and slowly pulls it out of her mouth.

"And what kind of hot am I now?"

I can't even tell an obviously distorted and overly sexualized mental apparition of her that it's an I want to fuck you, but I'll need to stop at an ATM first kinda hot.

She gets on her hands and knees facing me.
"Just tell me."
Well... to put it simply... you kinda look like a whore.

I shake my head violently to reset my train of thought and chase away this "slutified" apparition of Mary. I don't want to imagine any version of her, regardless of its accuracy, react to me saying that—even if it happens to be true.
A Sinatra song that I don't recognize comes on as I return to pacing around the basement in my normal looping zigzag pattern.

Now, who was it that told me Playboy is better than Penthouse, because it's classier or something like that?
I disagree, it isn't classier at all, it's just dishonest.
Penthouse doesn't need to lie about what it is and pretend to care about issues or make its pictures seem more like art. It knows it's meant for masturbation and doesn't care whether or not it's art; it doesn't have the need to justify itself.

Art or not, classy or not, a naked woman is getting jacked off to—by at least one man: whether it be the photographer enjoying unused prints, or the sculptor giving that armless statue a temporary fuckable pussy before the finishing touches are done.

Hefner may have done a lot for the porn industry, but I admire Flint's brutal honesty far more.

I don't understand how putting up a false front like that somehow legitimizes things. It happens with everything though. Most obviously I suppose would be politicians, they're always pretending they are whatever type of person they, or their advisors, believe the public wants them to be: family men, god-fearing Christians, etc. It's much too complex of a phenomenon to be limited to famous pornographers and politicians though. In all actuality, it likely permeates every facet of human society, every single one of us, and all of our interactions with each other.

If you really look at it—whether it is conscious, subconscious, or buried even deeper in your psyche than that there is an at least semi-definitive motive behind every interaction we have and why we include or exclude any given person from our lives. More often than not we hide these things from ourselves, especially when it comes to the people closest to us. No one wants to admit to themselves that someone they see as an important part of their life has that role due to some sorta ulterior motive, and while one can come to terms with their own motives when it comes to a friendship or relationship of any kind, it is much harder when you start to think about the motives those same people might have when it comes to keeping you in their lives. Only by denying this are we able to look at our relationships as if they are completely honest and true.

It can be hard to distinguish between intent and motive, especially when dealing in the realm of the conscious and unconscious. While every intention has some motivation behind it not every motivation infers an intention, and not all intents are simple and clear-cut. You can be motivated to spend time with a person for a variety of reasons.

Let's say they make you happy, for simplicity's sake.

So, you pick something as complex and abstract as happiness for the sake of simplicity? Not the brightest move.

I know, I know, but while it's something no one can put their finger on it is something that everyone can understand, or at least relate to.

Fair enough.

Anyways, there is nothing wrong with a motivation like this in its purest form, but complications can arise in the details. What about spending time with them makes you happy? Is it that they make you laugh? Do they help you forget your troubles? Do they help you to improve yourself?

And when we really start to consider what it is that brings about that happiness things can get problematic. If you are forgetting your troubles or boosting your own ego as a result of belittling and bringing a person down, this is likely a bad relationship for the other person. However, it is possible that they are motivated to spend time with you, because they get something out of being belittled, in which case things become even more complicated.

Weren't we talking about simplicity a moment ago.

You're not helping with the interruptions!

Sorry, go on.

Not only do you have to consider what both yourself, and the other party is getting out of the relationship, but this is also where intent comes into play. If a person intends to bring you down for their own benefit, but you actually get something out of it that they are unaware of are they really bringing you down at all? Are they really getting what motivates them to be in the relationship, or are you just providing them with the illusion that they are? Do you get a feeling of superiority out of this? And if that is the case, who's the bigger asshole, the person who intentionally tries to bring another down or the person who purposefully manipulates them into believing they're achieving that, in order to feel superior to the very person that's trying to bring them down?

Hold on! I think we've become lost in our own thoughts, and strayed from the initial point.

And that was?

Something to do with pornography, honesty, and purity of intent. I'm not sure it made any sense to begin with anymore.

I guess what it really boils down to, is that too often those who manipulate and hide their true intentions seem to benefit while other people: even if their motivations are negative, even if their intentions are negative...

Suddenly, I feel my leg vibrate.

Damn it! I think that was finally approaching something insightful, why'd my cellphone have to ring. Didn't even think I got any signal down here, especially with it in my pocket. Might as well see who it is though, once a train of thought has been derailed it'll never get to its original destination.

While turning off the CD player, I pull my vibrating cellphone out of my pocket and flip it open.

Chapter 9

Cross-country Bullshitin'

Hey, it's my brother!

I answer the phone and hear a staticky, "Yosh!"

"Hey man."

"Wha..."

A large burst of static cuts him off.

"Hey, I'll call you back on the house phone."

Somewhere in the course of that sentence the signal was lost. I head upstairs and my cellphone rings again before I can even grab the phone in the kitchen.

I answer it, "Hey man."

"Hey, what's up?"

"Not much... hey, I'm gonna call you back on the house phone this thing might cut out any second."

"Okay... I'll talk to you in a minute then."

"Yeah."

I flip my cellphone shut and put it in my pocket as I take the house phone off the receiver. I press the talk button.

Now what was his number?

Turning the phone off, I look at the bulletin board on the wall.

Could this shit be any more disorganized? Half of it is so outdated the paper is turning yellow.

I pull out my cellphone and cue up his number then press the talk button on the phone. I tap in half the numbers then hit off again.

Dumbass, you need a 1 before the area code.

I make the call correctly and he answers on the first ring with another, "Yosh!"

"Hey, what's up?"

"I can't get this MP4 to play, it worked before, but now it won't play at all, and I figured you'd know what codec I need to get it workin' right."

"Hmm, I know I had a similar problem awhile back. I'm not sure about the codec though, I tried a couple codec packs and got it workin'."

"You know what they were called?"

"Hold on a sec, I'll check on my computer."

"Okay."

I make my way downstairs and try to grab a smoke out of the pack in my pocket, but it's empty. As I grab my fresh pack, open it, and light a cigarette we are bombarded by chaotic bursts of static. Deciding that it's too annoying to bear I say, "Hey, hold on a sec. I'm gonna go get the good phone."

"Okay man."

I rush up to the second floor of the house to grab our other cordless phone off the receiver up there. While the reception of the kitchen phone is perfectly fine on the first floor of the house it gets progressively worse every step I take on the way up to the second floor. By the time I get to the top of the stairs the static is constant, as if I maxed out an old TV's volume on an empty channel. Once I switch to the other phone though, all the static completely disappears.

I say, "Alright! That's better."

"Yea," Dean agrees, but he is overshadowed by a loud beeping noise and asks, "What the hell was that?"

I fiddle with the kitchen phone trying to turn it off with no success. I answer over the continuous beeping, "The other phone won't fuckin' turn off! Hold on a sec and I'll see if hanging it up does the trick."

"Okay."

I make my way back downstairs and hang the piece of shit up then check to see if it's still on. "Alright man, we're good."

"Good, that was fucked up."

"Yea... Now where were we?"

"I needed the names of those codec packs."

"Oh yea."

I make my way into a now static free basement, sit at my computer, and take a couple drags off my smoke before saying, "Alright, let's see..." I pull up the folder where I keep a large assortment of install files. "Let's see, there's a couple, not sure which one worked though... there's the Combined Community Codec Pack and the K-Lite Codec Pack."

"I know I have an older version of the Combined Community one that I got from you."

"I have two versions of it on here, one from 2005 and one from 2006."

"Alright, I'll try getting the newest one then... You seen the Tenacious D movie yet?"

"No."

"It's fucking hilarious man."

"Really? The previews made it look like a lame rehashing of all the old shit."

"Does 6.3 some megs sound right for that pack?"

I hover over the file to see what size it is, "Let's see this one's 5.7, what's the date on it?"

"07 2006."

"This one's a little older, so that should be right."

"Cool... Yea, if you like Tenacious D you'll like the movie... It's more of a prequel to the show than anything else."

"Cool."

"You see any good movies lately?"

"Haven't really watched any movies lately, I've been watching more TV shows than anything else... You ever hear of <u>Odyssey 5</u>?"

"No."

I get up and start pacing around as I tell him, "It was this great sci-fi show on Showtime in like 2002, starring Peter Weller, the guy that played Robocop."

"Yea yea."

"It fucking pissed me off though because Showtime canceled it."

"Fuck them, the networks don't know what the hell they're doing... they fucking canceled <u>Lucky Louie</u>!"

"Yea, this really pissed me off though, 'cuz I thought it was just a one season show and the last episode looked like it was gonna wrap everything up, but then it ended up leaving more questions than it started with, like a typical season finale."

"Yea..."

"And I looked into it afterwards to see if it was based on a book or some shit, which it wasn't, and it turns out it was one of Showtime's highest rated shows at the time, but they canceled it since they didn't think it could compete with HBO shows like <u>The Sopranos</u>."

"No one will ever be able to compete with HBO."

"Yea, I don't know why though... I doubt I'll ever get into shit like <u>The Sopranos</u>..."

"Yea."

"...to me it just looks like a poor imitation of all the gangster movies from the 90s, just in TV show form."

He agrees saying, "Yea...," then adds, "I tried watching <u>Deadwood</u> one time, which dad really liked, but it went a whole episode without a gun being pulled... fuckin' western drama."

"I still haven't watched that one, or a bunch of the other shows I got from him."

I light another smoke.

When the hell'd I finish the first one? Doesn't say they can cause Alzheimer's on the pack, but it sure as hell seems like it at times.

Dean says, "Let's see if this works..." then after a brief pause he adds, "Sweet! It plays now."

"Hell yea."

"So, anything new with you?"

"Nope, just doing the school thing, playing video games, and fuckin' around on the computer."

"Cool. How 'bout with Glenn and all them?"

"I don't really see much of anyone these days, I run into Glenn at school now and then, but that's about it."

"What's he been up to?"

"Not too much..." I try to think of what has happened since I last talked to Dean then say, "Oh yeah, he quit his job a little while ago."

"Why?"

"I think he just got tired of slinging sandwiches for those crazy Indians. Kinda sucks though, 'cuz according to Neil they were about to fire him, and then he could've collected unemployment."

"Damn."

"Ferris got outta jail for the whole DUI thing, but I haven't seen him all that much since I haven't been going to the bar. Got tired of all that bullshit and drama with Tracy and him. ... That about brings you up to speed though. Not much going on these days, at least that I'm aware of."

After a short silence, he asks about our sister, "Anita still seeing that one guy?"

"Yea."

"I still don't understand how she could go from hating him so much to sayin', 'It was all a misunderstanding,' let alone dating the bastard."

"Yea," I shrug, "whatever makes her happy for the time being though."

"I suppose, but I don't like that fucker."

"Yea."

"I'm gonna let you go though, the girlfriend's coming over soon."

"Alright man."

"Later."

"Later."

"Peace!"

"Peace."

After he hangs up, I turn off the phone, go up to the second floor, and put it back on the receiver.

Chapter 10

The Child Trap

On my way back down to the basement, I grab another soda outta the fridge as the front door opens. My sister and mom come in carrying flimsy paper coffee cups. As I make my way to the stairs, I say, "Hey," giving them one of those half assed raise of the hand waves.

They both say, "Hi."

Without any further conversation, I head down into the basement cracking open the soda and taking a drink along the way. I sit back down at my computer, put the soda down, and light another cigarette. Compulsively, I check to see if there's any new anime to download, which there isn't. Hearing someone coming down the stairs I turn to see who it is.

My sister walks over asking, "Hey, how's it going?" and takes a seat in the beat up old arm chair next to me.

"Alright, you?"

"I'm alright."

I turn my attention back to the computer, and quickly glance over what I have to watch again to see if there is anything that she might enjoy. Unable to find anything, I turn to her asking, "So... what's up?"

"Nothing much, I don't have to work today."

"Cool."

After a momentary silence she slyly asks, "You wouldn't happen to have any pot wouldya?"

I knew she didn't come down here just to hang out.

I answer, "Nope."

"Damn, you got anything worth scrapin'?"

"Nope, I think you actually scraped what little there was left the other day."

"Damn, you're right."

As she finishes that statement we both hear someone else coming down the stairs and check to see who it is. My mom comes over excitedly asking Anita, "So, did you tell him the news?!"

She answers, "No! I promised I wouldn't."

"Well I didn't promise anything." my mom proclaims.

Anita tells me, "For the record, I didn't say anything,"

I give them both a, 'What the fuck are you talking about you crazy woman?' look.

My mom laughs and says, "Alden is like 'What are you people talking about?'"

Smiling, I say, "Yea, pretty much."

Anita chimes in, "You might wanna light another smoke for this."

I look at my mom and she smirks saying, "Yeah, you probly should."

I shrug and say, "Alright, I won't ever argue with that." I grab another cigarette and light it up. Anita follows suit smirking like she's practically unable to contain herself.

Seeing our cigarettes are lit, my mom excitedly announces, "Tracy's pregnant!"

I flail about laughing uncontrollably and slapping my knee. After nearly a minute, I stop and ask, "Is it Ferris's?"

My mom answers, "As far as we know."

"Poor bastard." I slap my knee a few more times and ask, "They happy about it?"

"Well she's ecstatic, I don't know about him though."

"Poor bastard."

"This is just what she wanted; now she's got him trapped so he has to be with her."

"Yeah."

Poor bastard. I guess the whole using her so he could get regular sex backfired on him, but I suppose he deserves it in a way.

My sister chimes in, "When Tracy tells you though, act surprised, because she wanted to tell you herself."

My mom adds, "Try not to laugh though."

"So..." I cough choking down some left over laughter, "I'm almost afraid to ask... they gonna get married?"

They both look at each other and shrug before my mom answers, "Not that we know of."

"If they do, and knowing the both of 'em, they will if they can go long enough without killing each other, that'll be one helluva unhappy marriage."

"Yeah." they both agree.

"I hope she doesn't think that everything is gonna be happy and great between them since they're having a kid."

My mom nods saying, "Yea, it'll probly end up getting worse." She pauses for a second before telling me, "Well, I just wanted to tell you that and see your reaction." Then, with a somewhat accusatory tone she adds, "but I'll let you two get back to whatever you were doing now."

As she leaves, my sister and I both say, "Alright, seeya later."

I shake my head in disbelief, and look over at Anita exclaiming, "It's absurd!"

"Yea, it is absurd."

"You know... I hate to wish bad things on people, but they would both be better off if the thing doesn't survive."

She doesn't respond right away, looking as if she wants to agree, but doesn't want to admit it—despite the fact that she'd probably have an abortion in a second if she ever got pregnant. When she finally does respond, she says, "Well, she did have a miscarriage when she was with Charlie."

I say, "I'd forgotten entirely about that..." then realizing that I almost sounded gleeful saying that, I clarify, "I don't think anyone should bring a kid into this world, let alone those two... together."

"Yea."

"Separately, they might make halfway decent parents ... but together, it isn't gonna work very well."

"Yea," she agrees, "they can barely go a couple hours without any drama and a baby won't make that any better."

"Yea."

"Oh, she wants me to be in the delivery room with her too." Anita cringes at the thought before asking herself, "Why'd I have to agree to that when she asked me months ago?"

"Lucky you, you get to see childbirth again."

"Yea, yet another reminder of why I'm never having kids."

"You never know, someday..."

Rolling her eyes, she cuts me off saying, "Alright, dad."

I laugh and tell her, "Sorry, channeled him for a minute there... at least I'm not as serious though."

We both sit around smoking another cigarette and periodically expressing our disbelief. After Anita finishes her smoke, she gets up saying, "Alright, well, I'm gonna head upstairs, make somethin' to eat, and take a nap."

"Alrighty."

She starts heading upstairs, but turns around to ask, "You goin' out tonight?"—meaning, 'You going to the bar tonight?'

"Not sure, I'll probably be at Glenn's."

"Alright, you guys should come out if you're not doing anything else though."

"We'll see."

Sounding disappointed she says, "Okay, seeya later."

"Later."

She heads up to the kitchen and I go back to blankly staring at the TV.

Chapter 11

The Drawer of Incriminating Evidence

For quite awhile, I just sit there staring at the TV and going over what to do in my indecisive head, making absolutely no progress at all. I light another cigarette and set it down on the edge of the ashtray, but it falls out onto the table and I notice that the ashtray is completely full. Looking around at the other four ashtrays in sight I see they're all either full or overflowing with cigarette butts.

Guess I better empty them.

I empty them out, one at a time, in the garbage can on the other side of the basement then plop down on my futon as I set the last ashtray back on top of the rolling end table next to it.

I've been meaning to clean out this thing for awhile now, I suppose now is as good a time as any. There was a time when there were enough drugs and paraphernalia in here to probably put me away for multiple lifetimes, but most of it has long since been used up.

No more coke, if there ever was any.

I only actually threw down money for it once and I doubt any of that made it back here. Never liked coke at all though, it just gave me panic attacks—and I've had my fair share of those without having to induce them with drugs. Freaking out, I'd just grit my teeth until it wore off. Glenn's ex-girlfriend used to do it all the time though and I never had the heart to turn down free drugs, even if I didn't like 'em.

I remember the first time I did it, she and her dealer had me snorting rails as fat as theirs. I tried my damnedest to keep up with those two seasoned addicts, and do my best to act like I enjoyed it. At the time I always prided myself on being a druggie and I didn't wanna seem uncool or full of shit since I wasn't enjoying it.

No more heroin, which I only briefly dabbled in.

Broke my syringe in two and threw it out of a car window by a park a long time ago—so some little kid could find and play with it.

I never much cared for heroin either. Snorting it wasn't too bad, but shooting up just made me feel like I was experiencing what it was like to be a zombie, and not one of the smarter neo-zombies you see in newer movies. No, one right out of the original Night of the Living Dead, but even less motivated than them.

I didn't even mimic their calls for, "Brains," as the junkies I knew did, calling out for, "He-ro-in," in half dead voices.

While I disliked coke more as a drug, the people and whole process of getting heroin was much worse. I'll trust a coke-head I barely know over any junkie, whether it be a close friend or even a family member. Getting heroin for us meant one of two things: trusting one of our junkie friends to get it in Chicago or taking them down there ourselves so they could yell out, "Blows!" or at times when a crack-head tagged along, "Blows and rocks!" In that city they have whole neighborhoods and networks of people dedicated to making the idea of drive-thru drug dealing a reality.

Both of these methods of acquiring the stuff were horrible ideas, but buying it in town was a sure rip-off while there was at least a semi-decent chance you wouldn't get a gun pulled on you or get ripped off by your so-called friends. Shit, some of the dealers even had promotions like find the black mark in your foil and get one free with your next purchase.

Anyhow, I only shot up twice, both on the same night, and the second time was only because my junky friend, and usual drug dealer, insisted I take another shot since he didn't think I had done enough to get the "amazing" rush that injecting it gives you. The needle was clean, from a brand new pack bought by someone's diabetic girlfriend, but it was a horrible idea to let a drunken junkie shoot me up. I didn't really know what I was doing though, and I'm far too shaky, (due to an unknown neurological condition I've had since childhood), to be able to find and hit a vein myself—so I didn't have much of a choice in the matter. I'm still alive though, and shooting it up was what made me realize how much I truly disliked the feeling of being all doped up, so I guess it all worked out for the best.

I still snorted it one time after that, but I didn't want to put it to waste considering that I'd already been horribly ripped off on the price. I didn't even really want it in the first place, but it was a chaotic night of drinking when I agreed to buy it and gave a couple of our junkie buddies the money.

You know how they say bad things come in threes.

Well, if you're like me and after 5 to 6 drinks your inner alcoholic takes over: you can lose an ounce of pot, break various glass objects, (one with your head), and get suckered into the con of two heroin addicts—all within the two hours it takes you to quadruple how much you've drank. I split the small amount of heroin I'd gotten with Ferris and Mary the next day, we all snorted our share, and that was the last time I did it. I don't intend to ever do it again.

I pull some empty plastic bags out of one of the drawers and check them for any shake that might be left over then start a pile of shit to toss out with them. I add a few pieces of tin foil left over from the one time I got crystal meth to the pile.

Now that was a good drug!

Of all the "hard" highly addictive drugs I did, it was the only one I could ever see myself forming a habit of using, and not because it left me wanting more but because I truly enjoyed doing it. For starters, I thought it was fun to do. There's almost an art to freebasing. Taking the lighter to the bottom of the tinfoil and inhaling the smoke through the hollowed out Bic pen, which I also used to snort pills and still resides within the drawer. Watching it all melt and mix together. Shaking the foil to rearrange it while the closer it got to being cashed the bigger and better each hit got. Every hit I could feel myself getting more fucked up as I held it in before exhaling, and it never gave me an overly fucked up feeling or the over stimulated coked up tweak out. Instead, it made me feel like I'd become some sorta cyborg, straight out of an anime, like someone from <u>Ghost in the Shell</u> or like I'd been <u>Technolyze</u>d. My brain worked with the speed and precision of a super computer, I could zoom in with my eyes, and I felt like I would be able to punch through a brick wall, move things with the power of my mind, and shoot pure energy out of my hands if I tried.

I never got a hold of any after the first time I got it though, and that's probably a good thing since I'd probably be fucked up on it right now. I can picture myself in some trailer park in the middle of nowhere, looking like a walking, slurring, compost heap while trying to spit my teeth out like bullets.

Having removed the tinfoil and a number of empty bags from the drawer leaves the majority of the useless leftovers taken care of. I add a couple unsalvagably crushed and torn packs of rolling papers to the pile before throwing it all away.

All that remains in the drawer is a variety of pipes, (some of which are broken, but I keep for some sorta sentimental value), various pipe cleaning implements from paper clips to pieces of coat hangers to two little switch blades each less than a couple inches long, and a bunch of containers that used to hold a variety of drugs over the years, (some of which still serve that purpose). Opening up an Altoids tin that's caked with resin I find the wrapper for the last mushroom chocolate I had.

Mushrooms, those are fun!
I've only done them a few times since they're usually hard to find and sell incredibly quickly. If you find some

that are really good and worth the price, which here in southeastern Wisconsin is almost always highly inflated, chances are they'll be sold out before you can stockpile any, or more likely the dealer will have already promised all he gets, and more, out to his clients before he even gets them.

Shrooms are pretty mild compared to most of the other hallucinogens I've taken and they are by far the easiest to handle. Also, aside from their hallucinogenic effect which is not much different than most of the other shit I've taken, though far less intense and overwhelming, they give you an amazingly unique body buzz—as if you can feel the vibrations of the entire universe within every molecule of your body.

I haven't really had any incredible, memorable mushroom experiences, but one specific moment always comes to mind. It was the first time I went to Bonnaroo, a 3 day music festival in Manchester, TN. I went with Ferris, Mary, a few other friends, as well as another group of people that I had never met and didn't much care for.

While Ferris and Mary were off doing their own thing, being lovers experimenting with drugs, I was left on my own for the majority of the festival. At the time, I was crazy about Mary, bitter that she was with Ferris and not me, and was just in a general funk since for the first time in my life weed wasn't agreeing with me. It was making me paranoid and anxious, but then and for a long time afterwards I still smoked it with the same reckless abandon that everyone else did. On top of that, the weather was horrible as it constantly switched between an almost unbearable heat and an incredibly windy downpour.

On the last day, I decided just to relax in the chillin' tent that we had, which was basically just an anti-bug screen with a roof, instead of walking around in the extreme heat and having a horrible time. I did, however, go out briefly to buy some gooballs to give to Anita and my dad. They were a mix of chocolate, peanut butter, Rice Krispies or something similar at least, and of course hash oil. The guy that sold them to me gave me a deal on his last mushroom chocolate.

I ate it and sat around with this guy that we all called "Cartman," who was like a real life version of the South Park character except not as angry; if he didn't smoke as much weed as he did though he probably would've been. We bullshitted for awhile and smoked a bowl to try out the chillum and weed I had bought the previous day. He smoked most of it since after a few hits I felt the mushrooms kicking in and was starting to get rainbow vision.

For what must've been a few hours we sat there listening to music. He was stoned as shit from eating a bunch of gooballs after he'd gotten the munchies from smoking a shitload of pot and I was trippin' balls staring at the tent, grass, and sky and watching them bleed in and out of each other mixing with colors that weren't even there. They teach you in science class that what we see as color is what light the object doesn't absorb, but when you're trippin' you see everything glow with those other colors. For quite awhile, the two of us ended up crouching down in our chairs and snickering as we watched a variety dumbasses, who thought they'd found a shortcut to the road, get stuck in the mud in the same places over and over again.

When everyone else came back, they fired up the grill and made hotdogs; I went over when they offered me one, but the menacing little grill stood between me and my meal. I looked at the grill and them, the grill and them, the grill and them, and they looked at me, all of us looking puzzled and confused.

"Come on." someone said.

"I'll frall in da gill." I slurred, having almost forgotten how to speak.

"No you won't."

I looked at the people I knew well.

"Just hand it to him." one of them said.

Someone actually aware of what it was like to trip handed me the hotdog. Relieved, I said "Thanks," and pulled my chair out of the tent then sat down by everyone making sure to stay a safe distance away from the grill.

After the mushrooms had kicked out of full gear I was pressured into drinking some nasty whiskey by the same jackasses who didn't understand my reaction to the grill. With a couple big "Fuck you!" chugs of defiance I made those bastards regret getting me to drink though, and they took the bottle away.

Anyhow, I take the wrapper, roll it into a ball, and flick it in the ashtray then light a cigarette. In an old pill bottle I find a small glob of opium.

Didn't think there was any left.

That's some good stuff, but there was only one time I ever smoked enough of it on its own to get fucked up and I don't remember a second of it.

Three little plastic containers, all labeled D & E Video Head Cleaner, sit hidden behind everything in one of the back corners of the drawer. The first contains the 5 or 6 video head cleaning ampoules, or poppers, that I still have left.

The liquid is black now.

That can't be good; it used to be yellow-orange.

It probably isn't safe to use these anymore, but what the hell, cyclohexyl nitrite was never supposed to be that safe to begin with, especially compared to the nitrites that preceded it, but are now illegal. After illegalizing the original amyl nitrite, the stuff in Raoul Duke's <u>Fear and Loathing</u> drug kit, it was replaced with a more harmful and less intoxicating incarnation which was illegalized and replaced over and over again. I think the indeterminate "they" finally gave up though. Amyl nitrite was originally meant to treat heart diseases like angina, but now you can only get its descendants under the guise of video head cleaner in bottles or the more traditional ampoules which come sheathed in plastic shells with piece of cotton at one end. It's inefficient to pop them and inhale the fumes when they're in that form though, so you have remove the shell and do as I do.

I grab the ampoule and the little bit of gauss I have left in the drawer.

You can use a hanky, or anything really, but I usually go with gauss since it's disposable. That way you don't have to worry about cleaning it up and you can carry a handful with you if you feel inclined to do so.

I wrap the gauss around the ampoule.

Now don't use too little or some of the chemical and/or some small shards of glass might shoot out, which isn't good since you will be popping this thing near your face.

I tape the ends closed and grab them. Then, holding it under my nose I put my thumbs under the center of the ampoule and push up with them as I pull the ends down with my index fingers.

(For the correct sound effect:
note the page number,
close the book,
hold it in one hand
and slap it with the other.)

I take a big whiff of the fumes as it pops then take a few more whiffs before setting the gauss on the table.

We used to pass these around and sniff on 'em for 5 to 10 minutes, but I always thought the best of it, the part that we were intending to get high off, evaporated pretty quick and after that it was the equivalent of huffing chemicals from under the sink, albeit a lot classier—but we were, I know I was at least, desperate to get fucked up back then. Shit, on a couple of occasions I even got a bunch of people to smoke a bowl I packed with a piece of fabric I had torn off my pants, and we all got giggly as fuck from smoking it too.

I become light-headed and that sensation spreads in waves through my body. I stare mindlessly at the wall for a few minutes watching the wood grain drip to the floor as it does even when I'm sober now in a perpetual acid flashback of sorts. After that, I remain slightly light-headed for awhile, but for all intents and purposes it's worn off.

Nitrites act as a sort of muscle relaxer and they are usually sold at sex shops. I've read that they work wonders when it comes to relaxing an asshole for anal sex, and if they're taken at the right moment they can supposedly amplify any orgasm to a level of ecstasy that few are familiar with.

The second container appears empty, but there remains evidence of what once was in it, because of the miniscule amount of AMT powder that can be seen clinging to the interior of the clear plastic.

I put away all the containers except the third, my acid stash, which I leave out for further examination.

Chapter 12

Hallucinogens: My Gateway Drugs

AMT.

AMT, not to be confused with EMT, a person you might need if you take too much of it or do something incredibly stupid and dangerous while on it—or if you carelessly mix it with other drugs or alcohol. While all of that goes for most drugs, it especially applies to AMT and its brethren of closely related hallucinogenic research chemicals. Just between the people I've met around here who have done it I've heard quite a few stories of trips to the emergency room, and one particularly interesting tale of AMT and a bottle of Everclear leading to a naked man being chased down by cops in a movie theater parking lot while screaming out, "Give birth to the universe!"

Now what's more in the spirit of drug experimentation than regularly taking large quantities of a research chemical virtually nothing is known about aside from the fact that it's hallucinogenic? Luckily though, the internet does provide you with a rough chart of dosages for the various methods of consumption.

Ferris, Mary, and I all threw down on the first batch we bought. It was sold to us as mescaline and that's what I thought it was at first, until I did some more thorough research on Erowid. Ferris and Mary knew before me, but they didn't tell me because they didn't want to... I forget their excuse, but I didn't really care. I probably wouldn't have bought as much as I did after my first trip if I'd known that though. If I took all the money I spent on AMT I probably could've ordered enough on the internet to rival the stash that our dealer had.

We picked it up on a Thursday, but since Ferris had work and both Mary and I had to go to school the next morning we waited till Friday night. The two of them had already taken their doses when I got a hold of Glenn, so he came and picked me up. After arriving at his house I put my dose in an emptied out Vitamin C capsule and swallowed it. Within 45 minutes I began to feel as if I was going to burst out of myself. Ferris and Mary still weren't feeling anything at the time, even though they had taken theirs first, but it kicked in for them shortly after it did for me.

As it kicked in, I stood up excitedly and paced around the room a bit trying to find a position that felt right, but that was impossible. Looking at the TV I saw the very familiar Mortal Kombat V start screen, but it looked completely different. I could make out half of it clearly, but the rest looked half tinted by a rainbow of colors and half black and white—just like Glenn's old TV did right after we took an industrial strength magnet to it.

How did the gays manage to steal the rainbow from the rest of us anyway?

Maybe in the future, if those thieving homos have their way, marriage will be an institution only associated with gays. They can have that though. I think straight people would be getting the better end of the deal if we got the rainbow back in exchange for that almost surefire destroyer of happiness that we call marriage.

But I digress, I looked at everybody and exclaimed, "Holy shit!" then feeling my stomach boil over I rushed outta the room.

I made an effort to look normal when I got into the hallway, just in case Glenn's parents were around, but when I didn't see them I ran straight to the bathroom. I slammed the door and locked it behind me then immediately plopped to my knees in front of the toilet.

Without any delay a chunky rainbow flowed out of me into the toilet.

Hitting the water this
                        pukefall
            splashed   drops of
            multicolored   fluid
                    all   over

my face.
            I took off my glasses

                                    and
                                    tossed
                                    them
                                    aside
so they wouldn't be sucked into
                        the vortex of color
                        within the toilet.

Looking around I watched the walls
move in   and out,
trying to catch their breath.
The shower curtain attempted to   break free
                                    from the
                                    small shackles
                                    that held it
                                    in place.
I gagged once

                                    then freed the
                                    rest of my
                                    stomach's
                                    contents
                                    into
                                    the   toilet.

With that done I felt a lot better, better than normal
even. Flushing the toilet I got up, picked up my glasses,
and set them on the sink. I washed off my face and rinsed
my glasses off then got lost in the mirror for a few minutes
watching myself and the room shift and distort as if I was
looking into a constantly changing funhouse mirror.
Breaking out of my trance I picked my glasses up; as I
lifted them to my face I paused to watch an unrealistic
depiction of the life cycle of the skin cells on my hand.
Once I finally put my glasses on, the uncontrolled blur of
hallucinations became clear. Looking around the room I
clearly saw the living pattern that everything was
composed of, and just by looking at it with different
intensities I could control its movements. I left the
bathroom smiling and feeling like a god.

The rest of that night has been for the most part lost in my memory. Those few short minutes in the bathroom overloaded my senses and by the time my brain could process and record experiences again, the AMT had worn off.

When our dealer showed up later to see if we were having a good time, I was so ecstatic and happy about how it made me feel that I arranged to get another $200 worth the next day.

Of all the other times I did AMT, probably somewhere between at least 7 and 13, there aren't many moments that really stick out.

It's kinda odd, while you're on it you feel like it's an unforgettable life changing moment that you could never forget, like you're being born again and not in that finding Jesus way, though most of those people sound like they're tripping beyond the point of no return. I hate to use one of the most overused clichés of my day, but you feel like you just came outta The Matrix and are experiencing reality for the first time. Things as simple as breathing and walking are new and exciting tasks that need to be mastered all over again.

I believe it was Ferris who said, "It's like having your soul shot through a rainbow!" And it does feel like your soul, if you believe in them, or if there is such a thing, has been altered on a fundamental level—improved. For days afterwards you often feel an unlimited appreciation for everything around you: from your dog's fly infested shitting grounds that you call a yard to that dead fish smell that all lakes seem to emanate. The feeling leaves you so gradually you don't really notice and often you never realize the fact that it was just a drug induced simulation of a mystical awakening rather than a truly life altering, permanent change that took place within you.

Anyhow, there were a few other moments that stick out a little more than the rest in the scrambled mess of my hallucinatory memories.

Making Mary smile with my tripped out realization of, "Wow she really does have a nice ass," a couple days after she had asked Glenn and I if we thought she did, revealing to us that she'd been self conscious about it since childhood.

The weird looks of Glenn's ex and Neil as while tripping balls I decided to make an adventure of joining them when she took him to show off the new apartment she had gotten with the guy she'd met and quickly married after she had broken up with Glenn. I made them stop at Arby's on the way back to Glenn's and bought five roast beef sandwiches for ten bucks since the 5 for $5 deal wasn't going on at the time. It's a pretty rare occasion that you get a craving for food when you're trippin', but when it happens the food tastes so good that it's hard to stop eating.

I let Mary have one after she had finally come out of hiding with Ferris in Glenn's room since she was having something of a bad trip. She was feeling better as the "bad" or most likely just overly intense part of her trip had ended. After we finished eating, we played chess for a little while on her trippy Alice in Wonderland chess set. It quickly became clear though that neither of us had the concentration to play a legitimate game of chess, so we ended up just randomly moving pieces around sorta makin' a new game out of chess board feng shui. The non-competitive nature of this new game was lost on her however, as she jumped my pieces periodically and won with a check mate that had probably been in place a few minutes before anyone noticed it.

Compared to everyone else that did AMT I was the oddball, having only one way too intense or "bad" trip, the bad part of which only lasted a couple hours. I'm not sure why. Maybe I had a sort of natural tolerance and didn't trip as hard. After all, we did all take similarly large doses. That theory seems highly unlikely to me however, especially since it often seemed to me like I was the most fucked up person out of those of us who were trippin', but then again maybe there was just more of a difference between how I acted sober and how I acted when I was tripping than there was for anyone else.

I personally think the biggest factor in my not having many bad trips, compared to everyone else, is that I've become accustomed to the panicky feeling that something is not quite right with me and the world. That sense that you are out of place in the world and that paranoid feeling that the people around you are out to get you, or at least don't like you deep down, those feelings and thoughts that can transform a trip into a bad trip are part of what goes on in my head on an almost daily basis.

I remember one time Ferris, Mary, and I all tripped by the lake. We chilled on the rocks for awhile and I was so fucked up I said with the utmost certainty, "If I wasn't this rock, man, I'd fall off myself."

Neither Ferris, or Mary enjoyed that trip very much. They said all the white noise of the waves was getting to them, but I liked it despite the freak out I was having in my head thinking that Mary might tell Ferris about the feelings we had for each other in order to get it off her chest. We had gotten him to trip when he didn't really want to, because he didn't want us to have the kind of bonding moment that two people tripping with just each other tend to have. When I tripped with them, it always became a bonding experience for them while I was the third wheel. It's a wonder I didn't have a lot of bad trips since most of the time I felt out of place, even among the people I was trippin' with, and I was always battling with my desire to be with Mary and my jealousy of Ferris.

The one "bad" or partially bad trip I did have though was actually the first and probably only time I did AMT completely on my own. I took it, strangely early in the day, somewhere between 3 and 4 in the afternoon, and around 4:20 Glenn and I went into his room and started toking up. Normally, at that time of day we'd've had to go for a drive to smoke up since it was winter and was way too cold to stand outside smoking in the backyard, but his parents had left, as they often do, to go out with some of their friends.

We smoked two or three bowls; after the first I felt the AMT starting to kick in, but stupidly I continued smoking—which served to greatly intensify the oncoming trip. Just as we were cleaning up and about to leave the room Neil knocked on the window. I took a few hits off the first of three more bowls then stopped since the AMT had completely kicked in.

I sat down on the bed and slowly looked around the room trying to gain some sort of control. It felt like I was hatching out of myself and everything was moving in fast forward, except for sounds which had become slown down.

A nearby clothes hamper periodically erupted and refilled itself in the blink of an eye.

One wall of Glenn's bedroom has always been covered in wallpaper that makes one huge picture of the Earth in the sky above the moon's horizon. As I looked up from the enchanting yet nauseatingly swirly carpet the Earth bounced around on the wall; it shrank and grew looking like some sorta screensaver. The clouds on it distorted themselves, making it look like a multicolored superball.

At that point Glenn and Neil adjourned to the family room but I stayed there, since I needed to gather some composure. As I smoked a cigarette pacing around the room and trying not to look at anything too hard, out of the corner of my eye I caught a glimpse of the Earth doing something even stranger. It started to come out of the wall.

At first it just looked like it was transforming into a highly detailed topographical map, but it soon went out of control. Spikes shot out of the globe and I dodged a few of the slower ones. Just as one was about to pierce my right eye the door opened stopping the hallucination. Glenn came in to get his cigarettes.

I decided I wasn't going to hide in there all night, as many people had tended to do in the past while tripping. In part, just because I didn't want to have to come up with some sort of excuse for being in there when his parents got home. So I followed Glenn into the family room. After a minute I managed to get Neil to give up the computer and started watching <u>Dragon Ball Z - Movie 12: Exploding Dragon Fist</u>.

For the most part I draw a blank from there on, but I'm pretty sure I just laid back in the computer chair, not really watching the movie, feeling as if I was a floating entity that had a small amount of control over everything in my field of vision, with the exception of the computer monitor. After the movie ended, the effects of the AMT had mellowed out enough for my trip to reach a normal level.

Right at the end of the movie though, something crazy happened. Maybe something was wrong with the file or it was meant to do this or someone rewound it and I was too fucked up to notice, but regardlessly the final clash that vanquished the bad guy rewound itself and played again the final clash that vanquished the bad guy rewound itself and played again, making me feel as if I'd made a small time defying journey.

How in the hell did my brother manage to buy a car and drive it home on that stuff?

The crazy bastard!

The only other research chemical I tried gave me probably the most intense, but short-lived and horrible trip I've ever had. Now, as long as I can remember I've always read and heard that regular DMT is supposedly supposed to feel like being shot out of a cannon for 30 minutes. I've never done DMT, but for me 5Meo-DMT was one of the most insane and horrible feeling experiences of my entire life.

For awhile after Ferris, Mary, and I smoked it out of one of Glenn's glass steamrollers I felt as if I was being turned inside out continuously. It wasn't like I was repeatedly being turned inside out and returned to normal over and over again. That would've been a lot better. It was more like being turned inside out then having the insides of my insides turned inside out and so on and so forth until my body was so scrambled up and in pain that I couldn't do anything. Now, I've never been shot out of a cannon, but if it's anything like that, even if only for a moment, I'll pass.

To make things worse, Mary was feeling something at least somewhat similar and had beaten me to the bathroom to vomit. Though it was only a couple minutes, when you feel that horrible and are holding in your own vomit it feels practically like an eternity.

The incredibly strange thing though, was that after an hour or so I felt completely normal until I did a popper and smoked a bowl with Glenn and Ferris. For both Ferris and I that kicked in a comfortably mellow trip, as if that torturous hour had eliminated the whole strange feeling of coming up and getting acclimated to the new world around you.

I open up my acid stash to take an inventory of what I have left.

There's seven hits left of one ten strip, another untouched ten strip, and slightly more than four hits in gel tab form.

That makes just about 21 hits of LSD and...

What's that?

Oh shit! I'd almost forgotten about that.

21 hits of LSD and a triple stacker of ecstasy.

Ecstasy, that's another great drug!

It's similar to acid, but instead of a visual head-trip it affects your body, primarily your sense of touch, but often there is a significant amount of overlap in the effects of those two drugs. As its name implies it makes you feel like you are in ecstasy, every little movement feels great. I've only done it a few times though and most of those times I'd taken acid as well which makes for a great time by the way.

Anyway, on ecstasy at one point or another even the most quiet and reserved person feels like dancing or doing a horrible imitation of a raver playing with their imaginary ball. This tends to give anyone who doesn't know what they're on the distinct impression that they're severely retarded.

I've been on both sides of that myself.

The one thing that I never understood though was the fascination people on ecstasy often have with Vic's Vaporub. Sometimes people will pass it around like it's a miraculous cure-all in a leper colony. I've always taken a couple whiffs, nodded my head like I understood what the hell the point was, and passed it on remembering why I hated the smell of it when I was a kid. I've seen people fight over it though, and sit there smelling that shit for hours on end. I suppose clearing and opening up your air waves might feel cool, I prefer filling them up with cigarette smoke myself, but doing nothing but snuggling up with a jar of Vaporub seems to me like a waste of drugs and good ecstasy is usually pretty hard to come by, around here at least.

I put the drugs away, counting the LSD one last time.

LSD.
By far it's my favorite drug!
The fact that I keep 21 hits around, so I know I'll have some ready whenever I want should've tipped you off to that fact.
In a way, acid was what got me started doing drugs. I had smoked pot prior to it, but swore not to smoke it again after getting some shit that was most likely laced with crack and/or PCP.

It was my freshman year of high school and I had traded some kid I had a couple classes with the remaining 8 cigarettes in my pack for three bowls worth of what I thought was regular pot. That weekend, my brother and I smoked all three bowls in quick succession, between just the two of us. At first, we were having a blast, laughing uncontrollably at absolutely nothing like we'd come straight out of an old black and white anti-marijuana propaganda film.
After a little while, nearly my entire body started to feel numb, and I slurred, "My whole body's dead... except for, this shoulder." Dean hit me in that shoulder and it went numb as well. As I laughed I exclaimed, "You just killed my shoulder!"
Hearing that, even the two sober friends that were with us laughed as if they were as fucked up as us—but the fun didn't last very long since my brother, fucked up out of his gourd and not knowing what was going on, took off out of the house. Our friends made me stay home while they

chased after him since they didn't want to have to chase down two fucked up people.

So for about an hour, I laid in the fetal position on my bed all by myself, tweaking out and having full body twitches while they chased him down and he fled hiding in the park by our house—thinking that one of them was a bear attacking him and the other was a cop.

Once they finally returned, Dean proceeded to alternate between going comatose, trying to escape, and sneaking off to try and hit the cashed out pipe. The first time he went comatose I freaked out and one of the guys said that he'd heard milk could help, so I hastily grabbed the gallon in the fridge. They stopped me from pouring it into Dean's mouth since they didn't want my fucked up ass to drown him, because I took their joke of a suggestion seriously. One of them administered some milk himself all the while trying to hold back his laughter, with limited success.

Once Dean had calmed down to an acceptable level and was no longer trying to get away when he wasn't comatose, our friends took off since it was pretty late and they had to get home before their curfews. Not too long after that, while Dean was in one of his mini-comas he stopped breathing. I frantically checked for a pulse and listened for a heartbeat, but there was nothing. I was about to start trying to do CPR, but with one, "Shit man, oh shit," hit to the chest he came to—gasping as he lunged up almost into a sitting position, and fell back to the floor. I got him to move to the bed instead of lying on the hard floor and spent a couple hours lying next to him and making sure that his heart didn't stop again before I went to sleep myself.

The next day we both made a pact never to smoke pot again. After a little while though, he started back up on a regular basis. I smoked once or twice with him, but I didn't really start seriously smoking again until after the first time I did acid.

Dean had left for the army and I hadn't even smoked cigarettes for over a month when a kid at school, who worked at Target with my mom and I knew since he was friends with Charlie and sat with us at lunch, sold me a couple of sugar cubes that had been sitting in his freezer for awhile. Each one had a hit and a half of acid on it.

I'd wanted to try acid ever since I was a little kid and heard about the hallucinations it caused in DARE class, and this finally gave me an opportunity to give it a shot.

The Friday after I got it, I took a cube after school. I left the other in an empty box of ham and cheese Hot Pockets buried in the bottom of our chest freezer then laid in bed fucking around and making some braindance music with FruityLoops 3. By the time it kicked in I had a 5 minute chunk of music done, so I put on some head phones and let it play. Waves of physical sensations flowed through my body.

For the most part my entire first acid trip was more like being on ecstasy than acid. I didn't get many visuals, but the closed eye visuals were some of the coolest I've ever gotten.

I closed my eyes listening to the music and waved my arms through the air. Complex tessellations materialized before me, swallowing each other and evolving. The insane music vibrated through me and a kaleidoscope of colors swirled around.

After the song ended I couldn't help, but feel happier than I had ever felt. I got up and felt what it was like to move around then danced around my room like I was at Woodstock or some shit, fascinated with every little movement I made, as if it was the first time I'd ever moved. My sister came down and I greeted her excitedly, "Heeey! Anita, man, I'm never gonna flick someone off again. Cuz you know? It's like a waste of such a beautiful feeling, moving your finger to flick someone off like that."

She laughed her ass off and I convinced her to take me with her to the nearby restaurant she was headed to for coffee. I had a fun time hanging out with her, watching the painting of clouds on the skylight as if I was lying out on the grass looking at real clouds, playing with my hand as if it was a toy, and smoking all her cigarettes away.

After that I started smoking pot and hanging out with Charlie, Neil, and Glenn on an almost daily basis.

Chapter 12.5

Appendix A

Since I'm on the topic of drugs I'll give you an essay I wrote years ago, in its entirety. For your convenience and in the spirit of shitting on the conventional literary structure, which I have been taught and has been the framework for nearly every book I've ever read, I'll save you the trouble of searching through the back of the book. Skip over it if you want, it's purely supplemental, but I think if you haven't thrown away or burnt this book by now you probably will find this quite amusing and worth your time.

"Only a couple of times."
"We were all thinking of quitting anyways."
Or
Why your Child Lies about their Drug Habit

by
Alden Baird
Originally created: July 4, 2002
Revised: 2003
Copied and Pasted: 2007

Few people can understand why a person becomes a drug user. After all, who in their right mind would embrace such a shameful lifestyle? Having an outlook like that, as most "productive" members of our society do, is the first problem in reaching that understanding. A druggie is not your typical human being with a headache, cold, or injury. They use illegal drugs and "abuse" the legal ones. Evil and without values these people will steal money, raid medicine cabinets, and/or molest our children while they aren't busy preparing to cook us alive and chew the tender flesh off our bones.

Or at least that's what kids are taught to deter them from trying drugs or associating with drug users. Throw in a few words like deviant, psychotic, and illegal. Then, name a few drugs: LSD, PCP, marijuana, and crack. Top it all off with cancer, death, and above all AIDS. Then, you're sure to have the little bastards pissing their pants even when they try to get tooth paste out of that precious medicine cabinet. This is no exaggeration, the misinformation about marijuana alone that is given out to parents and kids on a daily basis is enough to make one question the validity of the information we are given about lesser known drugs.

Meanwhile, drugs are becoming more and more necessary in this misinformed society that shuns them. Zoloft, Paxil, Prozac, Adderall, and other similar drugs are being instantaneously given to troubled youths after a ten minute visit with a psychiatrist. All the kid has to do is tell them what they want to hear and let all the blame for their wrong doings fall on a chemical imbalance. Hell, regardless of what the kid says they'll find a drug to throw at them. These drugs though, often don't work and are just "abused" or sold at school for pure profit.

Few parents, counselors, or psychiatrists understand the amplitude of the problems children have to face growing up in this day and age. We are the future, you won't let us forget that, and as a president Reagan once said, "This generation may be the one to face the end of the world..." Maybe he wasn't talking about my generation, but the generation he spoke of is still around and I find it hard to argue with that statement after watching the news lately. Everyday, we can't be sure if the life goals we have been taught to create will be cut short by a terrorist attack, or even one of our peers snapping and unloading a gun into us and the ones we love. The media makes this even worse by constantly shoving these things in our faces, adding to the fear and tension that is already almost unbearable for many.

It's no wonder these kids snap between all of that, the pestering they receive from kids that think they are better than them for whatever stupid reason, and the outrageous demands adults have for youths. We have to end up better off than our parents or we fall far below their expectations. College or a cardboard box and that's the biggest choice we are given throughout our whole life. Creativity is to be exchanged for productivity as we enter the "real" world and become a part of the machinery of society.

Drugs are the only escape from this never ending torment of day-to-day life. They allow their users to forget or at least temporarily stop caring about these things. The happiness that comes from this is not artificial as many would tell you. It is as pure and natural as any other feeling, and is the result of removing the mental barrier between the drug user and their happiness. Drugs enhance our emotions and feelings, but experience is needed to limit this to the good ones. Some people, however, are too full of paranoia and misinformation making them unprepared for opening up their minds. These cases are often turned into more propaganda for the anti-drug cause, adding to the paranoia and misinformation that the common person is filled with.

Our government has seen to this, filling people's heads with information about the evils of drugs in an effort to bring down people they can neither understand nor accept. Despite the impossibility of the Drug War's ultimate success it has had a lasting effect on the drug situation in this country. Drugs are not as easily obtained. The harder drugs are harder to get and finding a dealer is much harder than it used to be, because most people are more cautious. Most users from smaller cities are limited to marijuana which is less deadly than alcohol and strangely the drug that the majority of people worry about. Admitting to yourself that your kid tried marijuana is much easier than admitting they were "stupid" enough to try LSD or any other "hard" drug. This way at least you can blame it on peer pressure and their friends. You'll probably never know if they have tried any hard drugs because after seeing your reaction to their pot smoking they'll never tell the truth about anything heavier. With many of the harder drugs for the most part limited to larger cities the user in a smaller city must find some alternatives. A wide variety of over-the-counter products can be used: there is ether in starting fluid, DXM in cough syrup, and tons of other intoxicants that can be purchased at the local pharmacy, and can be more deadly than anything obtained illegally if the user doesn't know what they are doing.

Telling a parent the truth about a drug habit is almost impossible. Kids have enough trouble trying to get along with and relate to their parents without having to deal with this gigantic gap in ideals and moral values. Using drugs is unacceptable behavior, and most parents can't begin to understand and accept it even if they used them when they were young. Every time a kid gets caught it happens to be when they were going to quit or they never were really into it in the first place. They tell you this because it's what you want to hear. Why would they tell you the truth if it's only going to get them locked up at home? Besides, if you've tried drugs before and they know it, you explain to them that you were just experimenting which is as big of a lie as what they tell you, whether you realize it or not. Kids have no say anyway, if they come clean and admit to everything you give them a definitive list of don'ts. At least when they leave out some details, or lie, they have room for error the next time they get caught.

Now, I'm not pretending to speak for every kid out there, but if you've ever caught your son or daughter smoking pot, drunk, or under the influence this is the closest you'll get to the truth about it, because by the time they tell you, if they ever do, they will most likely have adopted your mindset. Very few of us can avoid conformity forever.

Chapter 13

Patiently Waiting..............................., About Damn Time!

Having finished cleaning out the drawer, I get back on the computer to check if anything new has come out again. Almost as soon as I move the mouse Glenn messages me on AIM.

Glenn: Hey man
Me: hey
Glenn: whats up
Me: nm u?
Glenn: waiting for Neil to get here
Me: cool
Glenn: you want us to come get you when he gets here?
Mc: yea...im suprized your actually gettin neil outta his house
Glenn: yea

I check on a couple different torrent sites as I wait.
Still nothing new, or nothing worth downloading at least.
I grab my bag off the floor and look through it.

Let's see, what do I need for doing homework over the weekend? Need to: read a chapter out of this book on writing arguments, read another 50 pages of the fifth or so book I've had to read this semester about the relationship of an adolescent girl and her mother as they struggle with their identities as minority women, and read the final 200 or so pages of some old British novel, (a so-called timeless classic), written by some highly overrated and long-dead author.

I take my notebooks and folders for school and toss them on my desk then mark what pages of those books I need to read with some torn up scratch paper. I jam them back in the bag along with some of my own writings that I've been working on then check D2L to see if there's an assignment for my other class.

The only assignment is a posting on the fucking discussion board. I haven't done the last three and I don't intend to make them up, or do any more for that matter. I've nothing but bad things to say about everything we've read for that class, which might as well be Sentimental Literature 101, and I think the teacher who's enthusiastic about the material for some strange reason would be as motivated to give me a good grade on a posting bashing the books as I am to write it.

Fuck D2L!

It's bad enough I have to sit through the retarded class discussions on this shit, but this douche bag wants us to talk about it on the internet in our spare time as well. The bastard is too lazy to carry around the papers we turn in too, so we have to submit them online instead. If I had more ambition I'd find a way to submit a virus with my paper and fry the cock sucker's computer.

I click on the AIM window to see if I missed Glenn saying he was coming.

Nothing, the bastard's idle now.

Glenn does have the tendency to come pick me up without telling me he's actually coming so I grab my bag, put on my jacket, and fill my pockets with the usual crap then head upstairs and look out the window.

Well, he's not here yet.

I set my bag on the kitchen table by my spot and look in the fridge out of compulsion. My chair at the table starts to fall over since with the 3 or 4 jackets I keep draped over it and my bag leaning against it there is way too much weight for it to hold. I stand there watching it fall and hit the floor with a loud thud then close the fridge door before turning to pick it up muttering, "God damn it."

My dad calls out from the living room asking, "What was that?"

"Eh, my fuckin' chair fell over."

I pick the chair up along with my bag, which I lay down on the table this time then look outside again.

He's not here.

Maybe I should check to see if he messaged me.

I head downstairs and check, but Glenn's still idle so I go right back upstairs and look out the window yet again.

Still not here.

My dad asks, "You takin' off?"

"Yea, Glenn's pickin' me up."

"Okay."

I stand in the doorway of the living room and look at the TV to see what he's watching. Three pundits or whatever you call them, jackasses full of hot air that get paid to argue about bullshit and rarely talk about any important news or have anything to say worth listening to, are going on about Rosie O'Donnell. Some bullshit about her leaving "The View" and being a generally un-American whack-job.

"They're still talking about Rosie?" I ask.

"Yea."

I turn around and look out the front window in the kitchen again.

Still not here.

Returning to the living room I say, "You know that show's ratings are gonna go down now."

"Yea, all the hype and publicity 'cause of her got people who normally wouldn't watch it watching just to see what would happen."

"Yep."

Fuck Rosie!

Who the hell would give a shit about anything that disgusting no talent dyke has to say? She went from happy-go-lucky closet homosexual talk show host to bitter conspiracy theorist bull-dyke. Shoulda stayed in the closet, it was better for her and any poor sap that watches her. Now all she does is discredit people of her gender, political affiliation, and sexual orientation.

I look out the window again.

Nope.

Quick head downstairs and check on AIM again.

Nope.

I pop back into the living room where people are still arguing about Rosie's character. I look at my dad and say, "I wonder how many important events happen that we never even hear about because the news covers bullshit like this for days and days."

The commercials come on and my dad says, "Come to think about it, they spent less time talking about Virginia Tech than they have about this."

"Yea."

"And before that it was the Anna Nicole thing."

I take step back into the kitchen as I say, "Yea, and then there was the whole O.J. trial in the 90s."

"Oh yea, that went on forever."

I look out the window again saying, "It probably got more news coverage than 9-11."

Jesus! What the fuck is taking so long?

I hear my dad agree saying, "Yea, probly."

Since we've hit a lull in the conversation I quick slip away to the basement, sit at the computer, and check to see if Glenn has gotten back on AIM. I organize some files for a minute as I wait, putting recently downloaded episodes in their proper folders.

You know, I was surprised when they finally found out who the father of Anna Nicole's child was; my theory was that it was her son who died not long before she did. And that fucking Virginia Tech thing bothers me. One asshole with a 9mm and a 22 shouldn't be able to kill 30 or so people—unless he's some sort of super soldier, real life action hero, or a fucking anime character. To my understanding many of the people just lied on the ground waiting to be executed one by one. Is that how low people have fallen, so afraid of dying by gun shots or box cutters that we just lie down and die? I'm one of the most mild mannered and conflict avoiding people I know but even I, if faced with the knowledge I'd die if I did nothing, would take multiple gun shots trying to stop the bastard. If you're going to get shot anyways you might as well make it on your own terms rather than those of a terrorist, a disgruntled goth kid, or some Korean guy upset over his first failed class.

Now I don't mean to disrespect the dead, but fuck those bastards! If they had any survival instincts at all they would've rushed the fucker and though a few might've gotten a gunshot wound in the process, that cocksucker would've been as screwed as a deer frozen by headlights in the middle of a destruction derby. And for fuck's sake, they're victims of murder and their own lack of resolve, not fucking heroes. Maybe one or two did something heroic, but just because you were killed in some sort of tragic event doesn't automatically make you a hero. If you don't do everything in your power to stop the fucker that kills you and the people around you, then you're partially responsible for your deaths. That is unless you're killed in a way that you don't see it coming or have any time to react.

In that case, you're just fucked. If there is a god greet him with a, "What the fuck?!" and a mushroom slap.

The computer makes the du-da-rink sound of a new message being received so I pull up the window.

Glenn: hey, you want me to just pick you up now Neil
        still hasn't shown up
Me: yea... wtf
Glenn: im on my way
Me: ok cool

Knowing that Glenn is coming for sure I light a cigarette and turn off the lights as I head upstairs. In the kitchen, I look at my bag on the table and mutter to myself, "Eh, I probly won't even open it anyway." then poke my head in the living room saying, "Alright dad, I'm gonna wait out on the porch."

"Okay, I'll seeya later."

"Seeya."

"Take it easy."

Opening the door I say, "You too."

As I walk out the door he chuckles at the thought of a retired man being told to "take it easy."

Back in the day, I would sit out here and wait for Glenn to pick me up regardless of how long it took. I'd just read a book or write somethin' while listening for the rattle of his old car, which you could hear from over a block away. Unfortunately, since that car is long gone I have to remain relatively vigilant as I wait.

I sit down in one of the chairs on the porch then almost immediately get up and start walking back and forth. After pacing around for 10 minutes or so, watching the occasional car or person pass by, Glenn pulls up. I take a second in order to confirm it's him since I have nearly tried to get into the wrong car before.

Once I'm sure, I go and get in the passenger seat.

Glenn says, "Hey."

Closing the door I say, "Hey man."

"What's up?"

"Nothin', you?"

"Nothin'."

"So what's going on with Neil?"

"Fuck if I know, he was supposed to come right over."
"Jeez."

After driving for a few minutes Glenn pulls into a liquor store parking lot.

Giving him a confused look I ask, "What's up?"

"Gettin' some booze... you drinkin' tonight?"

"I'll drink a little, not gettin' trashed though."

He smiles as if to say, 'You're not gonna have any choice in the matter,' then asks, "Alright, any pref'rences?"

"No, whatever you wanna get."

"Tequila it is! You comin' in?"

"Nah."

"Okay, I'll be right back."

"Okay."

Glenn turns off the car and takes the keys out of the ignition. After opening the door and setting one foot on the ground he shakes his head, puts the keys back in, and turns the radio on. As he gets outta the car he says, "Make sure nobody steals it," then closes the door and heads into the store.

A couple minutes later Glenn comes out of the store. On his way to the car he stops and starts talking to someone that I can't see since there's a van in the way. A moment later he opens the door asking, "Do you have any change this guy can have?"

"No."

Glenn turns and says, "Sorry man, he doesn't have any either." He gets in, tosses the bottle in the backseat, closes the door, and starts the car.

"Guy needed money for booze?" I ask.

"Probably."

"I'm done givin' fuckers like that any money, even change."

"Yea, I mostly use plastic now so I couldn't even if I wanted to."

"After being like Santa Claus for the bums of Atlanta I've been fed up with it."

Glenn gives me a weird look and asks, "What?!"

"I swear I told you about that."

"Not that I remember."

"Eh, we were probably drunk."

"Wouldn't doubt it."

"Well anyways, when I took the bus to visit my brother in Florida it stopped in Atlanta and the designated smoking area for the station was on a street corner in the middle of fuckin' downtown Atlanta. I made the mistake of giving 50 cents to one bum that approached me and seeing that, the rest of the bastards formed a fucking line. I was handing out handfuls of change left and right as I smoked a couple cigarettes."

"Christ."

We pull up to Glenn's house and seeing Neil's car parked out front I say, "Hey there's Neil."

"'Bout damn time."

Glenn pulls into his driveway, grabs the bottle from the backseat, and hits the garage door opener. We both roll up our windows and get out of the car slamming the doors behind us.

Chapter 14

Here's to Bitches

Glenn and I both look over at Neil who's fiddlin' around in his car searching through the crap that has consumed his back seat and even started to engulf the passenger seat. As he rummages around Glenn and I impatiently look at him, look at each other, look 360 degrees around us, and look up at the sky all while frustratedly muttering things like: "Hurry the fuck up!", "What the hell is takin' so long?", "Christ!", "What the fuck is he lookin' for?", "Damn you, Neil." "Come on already.", and "This is getting fuckin' ridiculous!" After a couple minutes Neil gets out of his car carrying his Nintendo Wii.

As he walks up the driveway I greet him with a, "Hey."

Glenn asks, "Where the fuck have you been?"

"Hey," replies Neil, "I ended up gettin' pot ahead of time."

"Cool."

We all head inside through the garage then make our way through the kitchen and down the hall into the family room. I toss my jacket on the floor by my usual seat in the corner then turn to leave the room before sitting down. Glenn sits at the computer and Neil sits on the couch lighting a cigarette.

I stop at the door and turn around asking, "Anyone want anything to drink?"

Neil answers, "No." but Glenn doesn't respond at all. He just stares at the computer monitor with great concentration as he tries to find something in his favorites list.

"Glenn? Glenn!"

He snaps out of it and turns toward me.

Motioning toward the kitchen I ask him, "Beverage?"

He says, "No, I got a water," and picks the bottle up off the desk to confirm his statement.

"Alright."

I head back through the house to the second kitchen that doubles as a living room. Glenn's mom and dad are both sitting there watching a movie on TV.

His mom turns to see who it is and says, "Hi."

I say, "Hi," and make my way to the fridge.

She turns her attention back to the TV and Glenn's dad looks up at me saying, "Hi, Alden."

"Hi."

"How you doin'?"

"I'm alright, you?"

"Good."

"That's good."

I open the fridge and quick grab a Mountain Fury, which strangely tastes almost nothing like Mountain Dew. You can tell that that's what they were trying to replicate though, despite the fact that they must've fucked up pretty damn early in the process. I close the fridge and give

Glenn's dad a nod of the head then leave the room. On my way back to the family room I pass Glenn as he heads into the kitchen to get some shot glasses.

Not paying attention as I reenter the room, I almost trip over Neil who sits on the floor in front of the TV hooking up his Wii.

Neil and I have a somewhat interesting history, but surprisingly we're still friends. We barely ever see each other though, since he doesn't really leave the house very often except to go to work.

Back during the first summer that I was hanging out with everybody Neil was involved with a girl named Helen. How he managed to stay with this girl as long as he did is a mystery to everyone that knows the two of them. She was a total bitch, constantly trying to transform him into someone completely different by forcing him to quit smoking pot, which was and still is his favorite thing to do. No one I have ever met has been as devoted a stoner as Neil has been over the years. In the early days, every time he smoked it would cause him to throw up, but he liked it so much that he stuck with it despite that. I can't even imagine how much you have to love being high to go through that on a daily basis.

While the majority of the time Helen limited her bitchiness to Neil, on occasion it would show through and be directed at all of us. After all, we did enable and encourage everything he did that she hated. One occasion in particular always comes to mind. Now she did have a good, if not great, reason for being a bitch in this instance, but that's beside the point.

We were at a house party she had thrown when her parents left town for a weekend. Charlie, Glenn, and Neil were all having a blast drinking and getting high for quite awhile until they all started to feel either sick or worn out or both. I hadn't been drinking that night , because I'd gotten wasted the previous weekend while getting to know "Mr. Fleischmann and Mr. Bacardi!" way too well. This had resulted in me blacking out and getting in a very one-sided fight with the sidewalk that left a pretty damn big scrape on my cheek, for all the world to see.

Anyhow, I was finally starting to be happily stoned when we relocated to the kitchen after hanging out in the backyard for most of the night. Charlie, who at least had the awareness and sense to get to the kitchen sink, was the first to puke. Immediately, Helen and all the preppy idiots that were her friends started complaining and scoffing at the idea that a person would have the gall to puke in the kitchen sink. How could her family ever wash dishes again? Surely they'd have to buy a new house now or at the very least remodel their kitchen.

Amidst the snobbish gossiping Glenn stumbled his way towards Charlie to get a better look. As he looked over Charlie's shoulder either the sight or scent of the puke must have gotten to him, because he proceeded to throw up as well—covering the back of Charlie's jacket, and a large portion of the kitchen floor. Glenn and Charlie both vacated the room and I tried to calm the increasingly frustrated Helen down as I helped her clean up the mess that they'd given birth to.

Then, just as she was finally starting to calm down, we both noticed that Neil had nearly covered the entirety of the kitchen table with a pool of vomit, only leaving enough room to lay down his head. I tried not to laugh seeing his happy, smiling face next to this enormous pool of filth, but Helen did not find any humor in the situation at all. They had embarrassed her in front of all of her friends and she couldn't keep a cool head any longer, she just snapped.

She asked me if I could drive them back to Glenn's house and before I could even answer she told us all to get the hell out of her house. I got everyone out of there and they all stumbled around eventually making it to Glenn's car, luckily we had all only taken the one car. We piled in then turned on the radio and chilled for a little while planning to wait till one of them sobered up enough to drive.

Now freaking out about it and kicking us out was understandable and could've been let go, but she went a little too far when she sent someone out to the car to tell us to leave. On top of that, she didn't kick out her preppy friends that had puked all over the front door and her parent's bed, yet she was so quick to get rid of her embarrassment of a boyfriend and his loser friends. After that, pretty much the entire gang hated Helen except for Neil who made up with and continued seeing her, and myself being the only person able to look at the whole scenario from an objective perspective. I knew that while she may have been a bitch about it she wasn't entirely to blame as we had pretty much forced her hand.

Anyhow, Helen wasn't the greatest looking girl, though she was out of Neil's league, but there was a sort of exotic Indian, American or otherwise, feel to the way she both looked and held herself. I never really thought of her as more than Neil's girlfriend aside from the occasional meaningless fantasy, that guys tend to have about any girl who they spend a significant amount of time around, until she confided in me that she had feelings for me.

When it happened, I was spending most of my time hanging out with her and Neil. She had taken it upon herself to find a girl to hook me up with. Initially, it was supposed to be a simple task since she supposedly knew a girl that was both perfect for me and single, but that was not even close to the case.

First off, the girl had a boyfriend, but apparently if she would've found me worthy she was willing to overlook that semi-important detail. More troublesome than that though, was the fact that she was nowhere to be found. All the while, Helen and I were talking online a lot, getting to know each other, and developing an increasingly flirtatious rapport despite the fact that we never saw each other without Neil around.

I was eventually introduced to the girl Helen was planning to hook me up with at another party consisting nearly entirely of preppy people and I ended up bumming the girl a cigarette. She was ecstatic that I smoked the same brand as her, which was Camel at the time, but I barely had a minute to talk to her and I never saw her again after that.

By then Helen had already told me over the internet that she was interested in me. It was a relatively normal conversation, at least as normal as flirting with your friend's girlfriend can be, when out of nowhere she changed its course.

Helen: Can I ask you a personal question?
Me: yea
Helen: You dont have to answer if you dont want
Me: okay ... shoot
Helen: Have you ever thought of me as more than a
          friend?

I sorta sensed what was coming from the get go, but I was too naïve at the time to realize that when faced with that question from a friend's girlfriend you should lie like your fucking life depends on it. Even if you're given that option of not answering, it's a hoax! If you choose not to answer you are implying that the answer is, "Yes."

I answered with the truth.

Me: yes
Helen: Do you still?

Being caught up in the moment by then I answered, and truthfully too. She'd planted the seed and I couldn't help but think it.

Me: yea ... do you think about me as more than a
          friend?

She waited just long enough to drive me crazy for her .

Helen: Yes

And it was all downhill from there, part of me knew I was in trouble, but I ignored it. I was all over her on a couple of occasions running a hand across her back right in front of Neil as I flirted with reckless abandon. There was never a time up until then that I knew with certainty a girl liked me, so I was pretty reckless in my pursuit of her.

At one point, I even went to Great America with her and a couple of her friends. I gave the guys a bullshit excuse for not hanging out that day, telling them that I went there for a friend from school's birthday party. When she dropped me off at home we ended up kissing, it was my first kiss. Things were looking up for me and her until I made one horrible misstep by telling her I loved her on the internet. I think that sorta scared her off, because not too long after that while everybody was hangin' out in Glenn's family room playing video games she told Neil about it through AIM.

Out of nowhere, he got up off the computer and stormed out of the room yelling, "Have fun with Helen, Alden! You fucking asshole!"

Glenn, Ferris, and Charlie chased after him while I hopped on the computer to find out what the hell had happened. Neil had closed the message window however, and this was long before AIM ever kept a message history, so I had to ask Helen. Let's just say that she told him everything for simplicity's sake and the fact that I don't really remember much of the conversation.

After awhile, Ferris came back inside. As I paced around trying to figure out what to do he sat at the computer and talked to Helen for a minute. I told him I was thinking of climbing the fence in the backyard and dippin'. At first he didn't think it was a good idea, but once he had talked to Helen for awhile he said it was.

With his blessing I got the fuck outta there in a flash.

In the course of my hasty exit I forgot the Australian cowboy hat with a feather in it that I used to wear almost religiously, but I got it back later thanks to Nina. Neil had bent it up saying, "He stold my girlfriend, I'll steal his hat!" but no significant damage was done. That statement of his always seemed strange to me though. Aside from the obvious idiocy of it, she'd made it clear to both of us that she wanted to be with him, not me.

Anyhow, I was almost home in record time when Ferris, who had been sent to bring me back, pulled over in front of me and picked me up. Glenn, Ferris, Charlie, and I talked for a little while in the car and based slightly on what I said about Helen leading me on, but mostly on their own anti-Helen bias they weren't really angry with me, but with her. The following day, everyone got in a chat room to witness Neil lynching me with text. Afterwards I had planned on disappearing from the group, for awhile at least, but surprisingly the whole thing blew over within another day or two.

Glenn bursts into the room, shot glasses in hand, and exclaims, "Let's do a shot!" as he grabs the Tequila bottle.

"Pour 'em up." I say.

Having just finished hooking up his Wii, Neil stands up and Glenn asks, "Neil?"

He answers, "No."

Glenn stares Neil down and gives him five or so "Cooome onnn."s before Neil breaks down saying, "Alright man, just one."

Glenn shrugs and says, "Well, that's a start at least." then pours all our shots—giving himself a double. We all pound 'em back and each of us lights a cigarette.

Chapter 15

Nintendo You Disappoint Mii

I take a seat and Glenn hops a squat on the couch. Neil stays standing, and fucks around in the Wii's menus with the controller. He shows us some of the things that you can do.

"You click here to play Wii games, this is for playing Gamecube games... Oh, check this out."

He pops open the panel on the top of the Wii and I stand up to see.

"Here's all the ports for the Gamecube controllers."

As I sit back down I say, "Nice!"

He goes on, "This is where you can play all the old games you can download. There aren't many out yet, but I have a few."

The list reads like a Sega Genesis greatest hits cartridge with one exception, Mario Bros.

Highlighting Mario Bros Neil tells us, "This one pissed me off, I thought it was gonna be Super Mario for regular Nintendo, but it isn't."

"What is it, the old Atari version?" I ask.

"I'm not sure, I never played that."

"It was a minigame in Super Mario 3."

He thinks for a moment, "Yea, that's what it is."

He leaves that screen and says, "Check this out. You make your own little character, they call them Miis, and it keeps records and stats, and gives you a ranking on all the games you play."

"Cool."

He makes a couple clicks and points at the TV exclaiming, "It's Glenn!"

"Holy shit, it looks just like 'im."

Glenn looks at it and laughs saying, "I'll drink to that," then looking at me he asks, "Alden?"

"Sure, but I'm taking it easy for a little bit after this one."

Glenn has the tendency to try and get you to drink enough with him to polish off an entire bottle within 30 minutes to an hour after it's been opened.

There's one thing I really hate about the Nintendo Wii, it's not so much the Wii itself, but the people that own it. They always want you to create your own Mii right away, as if it's impossible for you to use one that has already been made, or like it's such a state of the art concept that you just have to check it out. It's not that having your own profile and avatar isn't cool and all, but when you're with a bunch of people who've never played it before no one really cares about having a little character named after them that may or may not look like them. So you end up feeling pressured to hurry your ass up and the thing turns out to look so unlike you that you might as well have used someone else's Mii in the first place. What's even worse though, is when you do have multiple people who "need" to make their Miis and even just one of them gets OCD about it and takes 10 to 15 minutes to make theirs, only finishing that quickly because everyone else tells them to hurry the fuck up. The thing usually still looks nothing like them anyways. And what's the point in wasting your time making your Mii on someone's Wii when you rarely see them, let alone hang out with them long enough to actually have time to play any games?

After I take the shot with Glenn, Neil brings up the create a Mii screen and hands me the controller.

"What's this for?" I ask.

"So you can make yourself."

"Oh... okay."

Can't we just play the damn thing?

"There's all sorts of different options, just play around with it."

I spend a few minutes making one that slightly resembles me, mainly because it has glasses and short messy hair kinda like mine, but after I finish it I accidently hit the wrong button or somethin' and fail to save the fucking thing—so I recreate it really quick.

"Alright, that's good enough how do I save it?"

"Here," Neil says, holding out his hand for the controller.

I hand it to him and he saves it properly for me then asks, "Alright, whaddo you guys wanna play?"

Glenn and I both ask, "Whatchu got?"

"I have <u>Zelda</u> and <u>Wii Sports</u> which has Tennis, Baseball, Bowling, Golf, and Boxing."

Glenn suggests, "Boxing."

"I only have one controller, so we'd have to take turns."

"Well fuck that than."

I ask, "What can we all play with just one controller?"

Neil thinks for a second then answers, "Bowling and golf."

"Bowling it is." I say.

"Yea." Glenn agrees.

Neil says, "Alright." and puts the disc in.

He starts the game up, selects all our characters, and starts the match. He insists that we use the little lanyard on the controller so we don't end up throwing it across the room, telling us, "There was a reviewer I read about that was playing the baseball game and ended up throwing the controller right into her HD plasma screen, breaking it."

Laughing I say, "Damn, that would suck."

"Yea... that deserves a shot!" Glenn exclaims.

Neil tells him, "You'll take any excuse you can get to take another shot."

"You think I need an excuse?"

I tell Neil, "The only excuse he needs is a bottle that isn't empty."

Neil laughs and Glenn agrees, "Damn straight!" then asks, "You in Alden?"

"No, you're on your own for this one."

"Come on, you gotta drink to that."

"I'll be in for the next one."

"Alright." He pours up a shot, slams it, and pours up two more as I make my first spare. "Time for the next one!" Glenn exclaims.

"Damn you!"

Neil laughs as Glenn and I take our shots together. We all play a few rounds of bowling and a round of golf which takes forever since Glenn gets a ridiculous score of

20 some over par. You can tell it's Neil's Wii and that he's played it a shitload, because while Glenn and I are standing up and going through the motions like actual bowlers and golfers or in Glenn's case more like someone beating a person to death with a club, Neil just sits down casually moving the controller.

For some reason the ball always seems to drift to the left for us, in the bowling game especially. Damn half-assed game developers couldn't even make it work as well as that game that you play with a small plastic bowling ball.
What was it?
Oh yea... Xavix Bowling.

Once the game of golf is finally over, Neil hops on the computer and Glenn and I give the boxing game a try. At first we hold the controller throwing actual punches, but nothing happens and both of us are quickly defeated.
Frustrated, and on the verge of whipping the controller across the room, Glenn exclaims, "What the fuck Neil, this shit isn't working!"

Neil gets up from the computer saying, "Here, lemme see." and snatches the controller away from Glenn before he can do any damage to it.
He annihilates his opponent with ease.
"How the fuck did you do that?" Glenn asks.
Neil answers, "You don't actually throw punches, you move the controller like this." He moves the controller as if it was the handle of a whip.

Glenn says, "Okay, I think I get it." and Neil hands him the controller then sits back down at the computer. Glenn and I take turns playing a few more rounds and this time we beat the crap out of the computer despite the fact that all we do is pretty much do is jab it in the face repeatedly. After we finish, I set the controller by the Wii.

Neil turns around and asks, "You guys done playin'?"

We both answer, "Yeah."

"Alright, I'm gonna pack this up then."

Glenn tells him, "Go nuts."

Neil packs up the Wii and sits back down as Glenn digs through the couch to find the remote. He hits the TV/Video button a couple times then changes the channel to Comedy Central. The door opens just as the sound of the TV kicks in. The blaring TV is almost deafening since it always has to be turned up for video games.

Glenn's dad pops in and tells him, "Your mom..."

Glenn turns the volume down on the TV and asks, "WHAT?!"

"Your mom and I are going out to dinner."

"Alright."

Glenn's dad looks over at Neil and me then asks, "You guys know what to do if the burglars come, right?"

We both laugh saying, "Yea."

He adds, "Give 'em everything they want," then turns back to Glenn to say, "Alright, we'll be back in a couple of hours."

Glenn says, "Okay." as his dad leaves the room.

Trying to get Glenn's attention Neil mimes like he's puffing on a joint and after a moment of Glenn not noticing he calls out, "Glenn!"

Turning toward him Glenn asks, "What?!"

Neil continues to mime toking up as he asks, "Can we go smoke?!"

Glenn starts to respond saying, "Yea gi..." when his mom pops into the room.

She tells Glenn, "We're going out to dinner with Bill and Cindy."

"Okay."

"See you in a little while."

"Seeya."

Looking over at Neil and me she says, "Seeya guys."

We both say, "Seeya."

"Bye Glenn."

"Bye."

"I love you."

"Love you too."

She leaves the room then Glenn looks over at Neil saying, "Jesus ass, you couldn't just wait till they left."

Neil bows his head in shame as he says, "Sorry."

Chapter 16

A Trip to the Moon

We watch TV for a few minutes and listen closely to what Glenn's parents are doing, all but literally putting our ears to the walls. Upon hearing their car start and drive off Neil asks Glenn, "So, can we smoke now?"

"Jeez," Glenn sighs, "yea, just let me take a shot real quick," then pointing at the bottle and cocking his head as if he's posing for an advertisement he asks, "Alden?"

I stand up and say, "Sure."

"Neil?"

Neil shakes his head saying, "Nah, I took one, and I'd rather just smoke."

"Eh, suit yourself."

Glenn pours up a shot for each of us, and we both pound them down. Getting up Glenn exclaims, "Alright, let's do this!"

Neil stands up pulling out his weed and we walk out of the family room then stop after a few steps. Neil motions to Glenn's room then toward the kitchen, not sure where we're gonna smoke.

I turn around and ask Glenn, who's pouring up another shot, "Where to? Your room, or the backyard?"

He makes an indecipherable gesture then takes the shot. I look at him asking, 'What the fuck did that mean?' with my body language. The gesture is strangely similar to the gesture people make to say, 'Give me a hug,' except you have a confused look on your face and lean backward instead of forward.

"Let's just go in my room." he says.

"Okay."

Hearing that, Neil goes into Glenn's room and maneuvers his way to the other side. I follow him in and squeeze myself behind the door in position to take my usual spot. Glenn comes in after me and as I close the door behind him. He takes his usual spot near the window on the other side of the room, and I grab the blanket on his bed to block the bottom of the door.

Glenn stops me saying, "No need for that."

I say, "Okay." and toss the blanket back on the bed.

He cracks open the window and asks Neil, "Can you turn the fan on?"

Neil turns the fan to face the window and puts it on the medium setting. He opens his bag and smells the weed before asking Glenn, "You got a pipe?"

"Yea, which one you want?"

"Hmm..."

"I got those two small glass steam rollers, the T-1000, and a few other pipes."

"What others?"

"Well, ther..."

Cutting him off Neil says, "Nevermind, let's just use the T-1000."

Glenn says, "Alright, it's over there." and points at the book shelf that forms a sort of make-shift headboard for his bed. Neil looks on top of it and moves a few papers and CD cases around.

"Not there, on top of the books, in a pouch."

I warn Neil, "Watch out for his jit rag."

Glenn laughs as a surprised Neil looks at me asking, "You serious?"

"Yea."

He looks at Glenn.

Glenn confirms it saying, "It's true." with a shit-eating grin on his face.

I tell Neil, "I almost grabbed it once."

Glenn adds, "Nate thought I was joking one time and actually did."

As he backs away from the bookshelf Neil looks at Glenn and exclaims, "What the fuck?! You get it!"

Glenn reaches above the books on one of the shelves and pulls out a small black bag. He unzips it and pulls out a plain metal pipe then sets the bag on top of the bookshelf. He holds the pipe out to Neil and says, "Here you go, no cum on it or anything."

Neil takes the pipe, still cringing at the thought of touching Glenn's jit rag, then packs the bowl and offers it to Glenn.

Glenn shakes his head saying, "I'm good."

Neil protests, "Come on man, at least take one hit."

"No, last time I mixed liquor and pot I got sick as hell and woke up with my head in a bucket."

Neil and I both laugh.

Glenn says, "Seriously, I'm not joking."

"It's still funny." I tell him.

Neil persists in offering the pipe to him, "Come on, I took a shot, you can at least take one hit."

After thinking for a moment Glenn shrugs and grabs the pipe telling Neil, "Okay, but if I puke I'm aiming for you."

Neil gives him a dirty look as Glenn hits the pipe and passes it to me.

I almost hit the pipe then lower it from my mouth to ask, "Where's the boof tube."

Glenn looks around and still holding his hit in, he squeaks out, "Hold on."

He grabs the boof tube out of a box on his TV stand and exhales his hit through it.

For those of you who do not know what a boof tube is I'll explain. I've also heard one referred to as a mojo if that helps, but to me mojos are potato wedges often used as an alternative to French fries. The term boof on the other hand has only been used to describe one thing as far as I know, that being the act of coughing out pot smoke when you've taken too big of a hit or held it in for too long. Prior to the invention of the boof tube whenever we smoked pot inside we had to "ghost" our hits, holding them in to the point that we wouldn't exhale any smoke, but that didn't help when it came to boofing and in fact it made people boof much more frequently.

Anyway, a boof tube is generally a plastic bottle, or as it is in this case a toilet paper roll stuffed with dryer sheets. With plastic bottles you have to poke holes in the other end so air can get through. Also, you can make one with a soda can if you poke a hole in the bottom but you'll have to be careful not to snag your lip on the metal.

Glenn has his boof tube wrapped with tape to reinforce it so it doesn't unwind like a normal toilet paper roll. Also, he's added a couple small pieces of wood that he broke off of incense sticks. These are stabbed through the cardboard itself and held in place by rubber bands on one end of the tube so you don't blow the dryer sheets out. Regardless of what you make it out of, or how you customize it, the important thing is the dryer sheets. Shit, you could just poke a couple holes in a box of them if you wanted, as long as you have the dryer sheets to filter the smoke and fill the air with a spring fresh scent.

I take a hit and hand the pipe to Neil. As he takes his hit I blow mine out through the boof tube. He holds the pipe out to Glenn forgetting that he was only taking the one hit.

Glenn says, "I'm out."

"Oh, sorry."

Neil and I exchange the pipe and boof tube and after using the tube Neil sets it down on the TV tray that happens to be the only table with any room on it in Glenn's room.

Neil asks Glenn, "You think your mom heard me ask if we could smoke?"

"Probly."

Before hitting the pipe I ask, "Does it really matter at all anymore?"

"No, she's known that we smoked for a long time. It's just a matter of principal. She's cool about it, they have friends that smoke and shit, but I still don't wanna blatantly rub it in her face."

Neil nods saying, "Yea." as I hand the pipe to him.

I use the boof tube and put it back on the table before asking Glenn, "Remember the time that we smoked so much your mom had to come out back and tell us that your dad could smell it from in front of the house?"

"Yea, we had so many people out there smokin' that night."

Neil hits the pipe and hands it to me then grabs the boof tube, uses it, and sets it back down. He says, "I'm surprised your dad never knew."

"I think he was just in denial about it."

"Doesn't he know now?" I ask.

"Yea, but he thinks I don't do it anymore."

I hit the pipe, hand it to Neil, and all that shit. Then, I say, "He had to have known back then and just ignored it; he caught us in the act so many times. Remember all those times he knocked on the door to give us weird random shit that he'd gotten."

Neil says, "I must've missed that." then hits the pipe and goes to hand it to me.

"I think... oh I'm good... one time ..."

Neil cuts me off asking, "Whaaat?!"

"I don't smoke that much anymore, I get high really quick and if I smoke too much I end up trippin' balls or freakin' out, or both."

"Damn."

I light a cigarette. Glenn follows suit and says, "It's all that AMT you took."

"Yea, among other things..." I turn to Neil and continue, "...anyway, it happened at least twice that I remember, there was golf tees and..." Looking to Glenn for help I ask, "I know it happened more than once, what the fuck else was there?"

Neil hits the pipe again as Glenn says, "These things!" and holds up a leather keychain.

"Oh yea... was that the time he asked us if it was marijuana he smelt and you said it was just incense?"

"It might've been."

Neil gives us both a strange look.

I explain, "His dad knocked on the door to give us those things or tell us he was going to bed, or whatever, and when he was about to head off he knocked again and asked, 'Is that mari-juana I smell?' Glenn told him it was the incense and he believed it."

Neil laughs and Glenn adds, "I kinda felt bad about what happened after that."

Laughing I say, "But that was the best part, it was fuckin' hilarious."

Before taking another hit Neil asks, "What happened?"

Glenn and I both start, "We..."

He tells me to, "Go ahead."

"Alright... we waited a little while and all smoked a cigarette or two. Then, just as we were about to start smoking again and whoever happened to have the pipe lit their lighter, his dad knocked on the door again, this time to apologize for accusing us of smoking pot."

Neil laughs.

I add, "We were all crackin' up for 10-15 minutes."

Neil catches his breath and cashes out the bowl in the ashtray as he says, "That's great man."

He hands the pipe to Glenn and lights up a cigarette. As Glenn puts the pipe away he says, "Don't forget the classic story that someone always has to mention."

"What's that?" I ask.

He starts to say, "Don't you remem..."

Before he can finish I burst out with an enthusiastic, "Oh yea, that was the best!"

Neil asks, "Was I there for it?"

Glenn answers, "Yea, remember the time we were all smoking out back during the day and my dad came out to water the dirt."

Remembering, Neil says, "Oh yea, I had to hide a bong behind my back."

I say, "Yea, pretty much everyone had to hide some sort of pipe as his dad walked past us. We were all shifting around and passing them back and forth so they'd be better hidden."

We all stand around laughing as we remember what his dad said to us. Glenn says it out loud, "Then, as he was about to go back inside he turned to us and said, 'Watch out for the birds... they'll peck your eyes out.'"

We laugh hysterically. In between laughs I ask, "Didn't your mom call him inside and tell him to leave us alone after that?"

Barely able to speak Glenn answers, "Yea."

We all catch our breath for a moment and smoke our cigarettes. After a minute Glenn's cellphone rings and he answers it.

"Hello. ... We got me, Neil, and Alden over here at my house, you? ... Yea, come on over we're in my room right now, but we're almost done here. ... Yea, just knock on the window like the old days. ... Alright, we'll seeya shortly."

Glenn hangs up and puts the phone in his pocket.

Neil asks, "Who was that?"

Glenn answers, "Mary."

"Wow, I haven't seen her in a long time."

"Neither have I." I say.

Glenn says, "I think it's been a couple months since I have."

We all finish our cigarettes and put them out in the ashtray. Glenn scratches his chin and says, "I hope she's wearing a low cut shirt."

Neil laughs, but stops himself and shakes his head disapprovingly.

I open the door and turn to Glenn saying, "Now that's something I'll drink to!"

Glenn exclaims, "Alright! That's the spirit Alden!"

We all make our way back into the family room. Neil is still shaking his head as he sits back down at the computer. I pour up the shots this time, we clink them together, slam 'em, and take our seats.

Chapter 17

Mary (and Some Less Important Girls)

We all sit around for a little while waiting for Mary to show up. Neil fucks around on the computer, Glenn tries to find something to watch on TV, and I...

I think about Mary.

Mary.

It's hard for me to even think about her in any coherent way. I always end up getting lost in some sorta fantasy world where the two of us are the only people, or at least the only important characters. So, I'll try to start with when I met her and through a series of tangents I'll hopefully create a pretty good picture of our relationship to each other over the years and among other things how I feel about her, which is in many ways a mystery to me that I've never been able to solve.

When Ferris first brought Mary around most of us didn't want to even like her, let alone accept her into our group of friends. It was no fault of her own, but Ferris had imposed upon himself a break from smoking pot since she didn't smoke back then and he didn't want to make her feel out of place. At first, we all thought he was doing this, because she didn't want him to smoke at all much like Helen had done with Neil throughout the duration of their relationship.

Anyhow, when I first met her I thought she was hot, especially since she had red hair, albeit dyed red hair, but I've never seen it any other color so it might as well be naturally red. Strangely though, in the beginning I didn't even consider her as a potential girlfriend/lover despite the fact that I've had a thing for redheads ever since grade school.

There was this girl, Kathy, who was in the enrichment program with me from third through sixth grade. The moment I saw her I instantly developed a huge crush on her. She had long, natural and naturally curly red hair and the prettiest face I'd ever seen with just the right amount of freckles on her cheeks. Every other crush I'd had up until that moment had been your stereotypical young boy wanting to marry his teacher sorta thing, but this was my first true crush. The two of us hung out with the same group of kids and became pretty close friends. We were probably closer than any of the people who were actually dating at the time, but to my dismay it never developed into anything more than friendship.

Later on, after we'd both started going to different junior high schools we kept in touch for awhile, talking over the phone here and there. On a couple of occasions I even rode my bike over to her house so we could hang out. One night on the phone we got around to talking about how I'd never had a girlfriend. She told me how good of a guy I was and that I was good looking, then she basically told me that if there was a girl I liked I should just ask her out. She explained, "The girl would have to be crazy if she said no and it'd be her loss if she did."

I took this as a hint that I should just ask her out since she'd have to have been incredibly stupid if she didn't know that I liked her and I knew her to be a damn smart girl. So, I asked her out and she said yes. I was ecstatic for a whole week. I'd finally landed the girl I'd liked and wanted to be with for four years, but I couldn't get a hold of her that whole week since having just made her school's cheerleading squad she was busy with practice, or so she said.

The next weekend, when I called her she was at the movies with one of the guys that we'd gone to elementary school with. We had planned to go to the movies the weekend before, but she'd blown me off to go with him.

I was crushed...

Then, the following Monday, a girl we both knew from elementary school broke up with me on Kathy's behalf. I had no clue why until years later when one of our classmates who had moved away came back to town to visit everyone and we had reunion of sorts.

At the earliest opportunity I had, I asked Kathy, "Why'd you break up with me back then?"

She looked dumbfounded as she tried to remember what I was talking about. Then, when it finally clicked she nonchalantly said, "Oh that, that was just an over the phone thing."

I never considered it having a girlfriend after she'd broken up with me, since we were "going out" for all of a week and we'd never even talked once during that time period, but that confirmed it. How the hell can anyone date solely over the phone anyways? Furthermore, if your relationship is "just an over the phone" relationship and the break up takes place in person, whether they do the breaking up or not, does it count? After all, it didn't take place in the imaginary world of the telephone.

All that aside, I suppose she ended that punch-line-lacking joke of a relationship, because I was too needy of a phone boyfriend. I called a couple times on most days never getting a hold of her. People often say, "Long distance relationships never work." Well, when you're that young I guess the other side of town is a pretty long distance. The whole dating over the phone thing still throws me for a loop though; maybe Kathy wasn't nearly as smart as I gave her credit for, but then again I have always been incredibly bad at reading the intentions of women, especially in relation to me.

Anyhow, the main reason I didn't look at Mary that way was because I had a prospect of my own for the first time in years. Being an avid fan of anime as well as cosplay girls I'd take blue hair over red any day and even better than blue or red hair is their synergy as purple. That was the color of Ivy's hair and she was Asian or at least of predominantly Asian ancestry to boot. Not that nationality is a factor in whether or not I find someone attractive, but she had that whole J-Pop goth-punk look about her. For some reason, that look has turned me on for as long as I can remember, despite the fact that I am severely turned off by the tattoos which often come with it.

But I digress, I went to high school with Ivy and even though she was a year ahead of me we had a couple of classes together. She paid me some cash to do a crap-load of late math assignments for her and not long after that we started hanging out at lunch. We exchanged AIM screen names and for a couple of weeks we talked till the wee hours of the morning on an almost daily basis. During that time period we got together outside of school on two occasions.

The first time, we went to coffee with her cousin and her cousin's boyfriend. We tried to go bowling afterwards, but we couldn't get a lane so we dropped the other two off somewhere and went by the lake to sit and talk. Up until that point the whole night was a bust, I had been incredibly nervous and quiet the whole time, but things came much more naturally when it was just the two of us and we got to talking. Later, when she dropped me off at home we made out for a little while and that was the second time I'd ever kissed a girl, it hasn't happened since.

That was over five years ago.

A week later we hung out again, this time at her house. Once again the cousin and cousin's boyfriend, who by the way was a total douche bag, were both there. We all watched one of the girls' favorite movies, a true "classic" starring Clint Howard, The Ice Cream Man. I'd seen it on late night TV before and it was among the worst movies I'd ever seen, but I said it was pretty good just to humor them. I thought I was being slick putting my arm around her as we watched the movie, but it was more comical than anything else due to the fact that the girls were watching their assholish 5 to 6 year old cousin and he kept toying with my hand.

Ivy had wanted to dye my hair and I'd told her if I was to dye it any color it'd be blue.

Or was it green?

I don't exactly remember, but it doesn't really matter since she'd gotten the dye, but gave me the option to back out at the last minute and I took it. I have a feeling by doing that I failed some sort of 'Can I change him into who I want him to be?' test. When she dropped me off at home I went to kiss her, but she wouldn't let me. She came up with some retarded excuse of how she was on some sort of fast: from cigarettes, from weed, from alcohol, from meat, and most importantly from any sort of sexual activity in which kissing was included—though I swear she had smoked a cigarette or two earlier in the night.

After that I didn't hear from Ivy for a couple of weeks. We didn't even talk on the internet. The next time I saw her was during lunch at the school on Valentine's Day. She was all excited about her Valentine's plans to surprise her new boyfriend. Something that involved: roses, chocolate, and whip cream or some shit. I was tuning most of it out so I never got all the details. I was kinda preoccupied thinking about how odd it was that she had a boyfriend since she'd told me she wasn't looking for a relationship. I suppose she just left out the fact that she just wasn't looking for a relationship with me. She later told me she wasn't the girl for me, because if we would have gotten together she would've ended up hurting me and ruining me for some other girl that women keep telling me I'm bound to end up with... someday.

What a crock of mother fucking shit!

She still hurt me, but even though I haven't even kissed a girl since it's not because of her. Any girl has to be way too damn full of herself to honestly think she could ruin a guy for all other women. Anyone that can be ruined by someone like that should just lie down and die 'cause they're going to be miserable for the rest of their life.

Anyway, to cleanse my mind of Ivy and that whole frustrating and somewhat depressing ordeal I decided to dex, or robo trip if you will. Strangely, this led to one of the occasions that got Mary considering the possibility of dating me before she and Ferris had even officially gotten together.

Pay attention kids, you know how when you were little and your parents had to force you to take just a single dose of that nasty cough syrup. Well, if you drink somewhere between four and eight ounces of the stuff you'll have a fucking great time. I prefer Robitussin Maximum Strength: Cough, but anything with dextromethorphan as the only active ingredient will do the trick.

I arranged with Neil to go over to his place after school and told him I was going to dex, welcoming him to join me. We'd done it so many times by then though that he and everyone else were pretty tired of it. So, after school I stopped and got a bottle of cough syrup then downed it in the park behind our local fire station. When I got to Neil's he wasn't there, but the door was open and after a quick search of the house he and Glenn pulled up just as I was about to leave. Since no one was going to be home till late that night, we all went straight into the basement and proceeded to get stoned as fuck.

By the time Ferris showed up with Mary I was fucking blasted. Jumping all over the place I rambled on about how I needed to dex every few months in order to keep in touch with Mr. Universe, the incredibly unimaginative personification of the universe itself. Apparently, my drug induced energy and excitement made a good impression on her though, because that was the only specific moment she mentioned when she told me she'd liked me.

That moment came on one of the first occasions that Mary hung out with us without Ferris around. This only happened because he had to pick up an ounce or so of pot and the dealer didn't have it handy so Ferris ended up having to take him on a nearly three hour drive to go pick it up. Mary stayed behind at Glenn's house with Glenn and me since Ferris couldn't be certain he would be back in time to get her home before her curfew. The three of us sat around in the backyard bullshitting for quite awhile. This is when Mary told us that she was insecure about her ass and bent over when Glenn asked her to, so we could get a better look. We both agreed she had a nice ass and she thanked us even though she didn't really believe we were being honest.

Somehow, she got to talking about how it was cool to be hanging out with us without Ferris, since she was tired of always being the second half of Ferris and Mary or just Ferris's girlfriend, instead of simply Mary. She often felt as if she wasn't really part of the group and was just tagging along at Ferris's side. We assured her that she was our friend and that we didn't just hang out with her because she was going out with Ferris. Hearing that made her feel better, but she still seemed somewhat bitter toward Ferris as she let us in on a little secret; he actually wasn't even her first choice when she'd started hanging out with us before they were officially dating, but: it was easier and less complicated for her to date him, he was a close second or some shit like that, and she didn't want to rock the boat since he was the one bringing her around and courting her or whatever you wanna call it.

Glenn and I were taken aback by this revelation; we never even considered that she might've been into someone other than Ferris. We'd figured from day one the only reason she'd come around and hung out with us at all was because we were Ferris's friends and she wanted to get to know us since she liked him. Even more surprising was the idea that she had a choice and could've taken her pick of any of us. Granted, she could've had her pick of any of us, but many of us only knew her through Ferris and if she hadn't hooked up with him most of us would probably have never seen her again, let alone gotten to hang out with her long enough to get to know her and truly become friends.

Ferris is a good guy and all, but I doubt he'd continue to bring around a girl he wanted to hook up with in order to hook her up with a friend. You'd have to be some sort of completely pure and good person like: the Dalai Lama, Buddha, or Jesus to do something like that, (not just someone who resembles the stereotypical depiction of Jesus as Ferris does), and while those people might exist or might have existed in the past no one is or has ever been completely pure and good.

Anyway, we asked her who it was, but she wouldn't tell us. So, we started guessing even though she said she probably wouldn't say that we were right if we did guess who. We went through just about everyone that we hung out with, even people that weren't around very often at all.

"Neil?"

"No."

"Charlie?"

"No."
"Conrad?"
"Nope."
"Nick."
"No!"
"Lenny?"
"Nah."
"Nate?"
"No!"

It went on awhile longer until being exhausted of names outside of Glenn and myself, I asked, "Glenn?"

She answered, "No," then looking at Glenn she added, "sorry Glenn."

"It's alright, didn't even consider it a possibility so I didn't think to even ask."

Knowing my name was coming next, I got up from my seat on the steps and asked, "Anyone need anything to drink?"

"No." Glenn responded.

"No thanks." Mary said with a smile.

I made my way inside to get a soda and took my sweet ass time getting it from the fridge. I'm not sure exactly why I didn't wanna know the answer she'd give when asked my name. Part of it was that I did not want to get reeled into the whole friend's girlfriend love triangle thing since I knew that despite my past experiences and what they'd taught me I just wouldn't be able to resist making a play for her if she did like me—especially since it would almost be like Ferris stole away the one amazing girl I could've had a shot with. At least that's how I'd later try to justify it to myself. Another part of me didn't want to know, because I already liked her a lot and had a huge crush on her. For quite some time we'd been exchanging smiles from across the room whenever we'd catch each other looking at one another. I would often fantasize about her and Ferris breaking up and the two of us hooking up shortly afterwards. I didn't want to hear her say, "No," if it turned out to be someone we hadn't thought of, or if she had lied when answering us earlier. I desperately wanted to avoid having that fantasy of mine crushed under the force of reality.

Once I'd gotten my soda and started to make my way back outside I almost ran into Glenn who was standing up and about to go inside to use the bathroom or somethin'.

As we passed each other he told Mary, "Wow, don't worry I won't say anything."

"Thanks."

I sat on the steps and once Glenn went inside Mary asked me, "I told Glenn, do you wanna know?"

She wanted me to know. So, despite my better judgment I said, "Sure."

"It was you."

We both gave each other a big embarrassed smile.

Surprised, not so much by what she said but that she said it I asked, "Really?!"

She shyly answered, "Yup." all the while smiling.

Curious as to what I did to make her interested in me and hoping that I might be able to use whatever it was in future endeavors, whether it be with her or another girl, I asked, "Any particular reason why?"

She mentioned that one time I was dexing, though I don't remember the context, as I was kinda in shock the whole time she spoke. I do however remember that she liked how while I did not say much very often, whenever I did speak it was something either: intelligent, witty, or funny.

The conversation was cut short as Glenn came back out and we all talked about other shit for awhile until Ferris returned and we all got high as hell. After that Mary and I got to talking on AIM, fucking AIM, and so began as Ferris later put it, "Mary's emotional cheating" on him with me. Actually, I think the phrase originally came from Charlie referring to Tracy and me, but it fits my relationship with Mary much more accurately.

It wasn't my fault that he wasn't there for her enough emotionally; it's not like she was overly demanding in that department. He was practically out of town or in another country when it came to their emotional relationship though. More accurately, he was in the world of Diablo 2 and because of that it seemed to me like their relationship was on the expressway to self destruction.

She fucking hated Diablo 2 with a passion and everyone knew it, but that never deterred Ferris from playing it and ignoring her to play it. Ferris has had a card I've often seen him use to basically let him do whatever he wants and treat a girlfriend as he pleases; it's the, "Hey! You're supposed to be the cool girlfriend." card. With that, basically any grievance, even completely legitimate ones, can be pushed aside and ignored as if the girl was just being a bitchy drama queen. It seems to work pretty much flawlessly on any girl that prides herself on not being "one of those girls."

Anyhow, he'd pick her up, take her to his place, and play Diablo 2. Then, he'd turn on his MephBot, (a program that would take control of his sorceress, repeatedly kill the boss Mephisto, and pick up good gear when it dropped), fuck Mary, and go back to the computer to either watch the bot or hop on one of his many other characters. Later, at Glenn's house the first chance Ferris got he'd hop on <u>Diablo 2</u> and play some more.

I, on the other hand, did what he should've done, and dropped playing <u>Diablo 2</u> whenever she was around in order to devote my attention to her whether it be: to talk, listen to her play guitar and sing, play chess, let her read something I'd written, or simply look at her and smile.

Chapter 17.5

Appendix B

The following is a love poem I wrote for Mary. At the time I was dabbling in poetry, mostly depressing or humorously perverted stuff. I'd let her read my poems whenever she felt like it. Upon reading this one, she immediately knew I'd written it for her. She liked it a lot and would ask me if she could read my poems or just grab the notebook nearly every time I saw her, just to read this poem. After awhile, when Nina and Tracy became curious to read my poetry this one was separated into its own section of the notebook which I only let Mary read. Ferris, knowing something was up, would often fuck with me, grabbing the notebook and asking, "Which ones can't I read?" but he always gave it back and never read a thing.

In retrospect, it makes me feel stupid when I remember how great I thought this poem was and that if I whispered it in her ear she would melt my arms. Looking at it as a poem I don't even think it's any good, though it may have some potential, but when you're love struck, or whatever you wanna call it, any expression of that feeling feels like it's pure genius. (I still like the end though).

"If I could whisper in your ear."

Sweet beautiful girl,
I long to hold your hand,
To feel the softness of your skin,
And gaze into your mystifying eyes,
For mine shed tears without your beauty to sooth them.
Your voice hits my ears like a sweet melody,
And wherever you go you leave the smell of paradise.
I can't help but smile when I'm with you,
You bring pleasure to all of my senses.
I only wish I could taste you.

Chapter 17 (Cont'd)

Mary (and an Even Less Important Girl)

Mary and I hung out by ourselves only one time back in those days. Ferris would've had to have been an idiot though, if he didn't know that something was up—due to the fact that Mary was willing to take a long bus ride with multiple transfers just to get out of the house a little early and hang out with me, while he was at work. Even more suspicious though was the fact that she felt as if she needed to get his permission to do it. If it was just hanging out with a friend I don't think she'd have felt that was necessary. That just screamed out she was trying cover her own ass, so if he got all pissed about it she could say, "Well, you said I could." like some sort of child manipulating its parents. If there was nothing to hide and be ashamed of I think it would've been natural to just let him know about it so he didn't get worried when he went to pick her up and she wasn't there.

It was sort of a pathetic occasion though, since both of us had very shy, quiet, and reserved personalities at the time—we both still do to a certain extent. Also, we both were holding ourselves back, because we felt somewhat guilty just for hanging out and would've felt even worse if anything actually happened. I can't speak for her, but I can say with certainty that the whole time I was hoping something would.

Anyway, we went for a walk along the beach and talked a little here and there, unsure of what to say or how to act around each other in that unfamiliar situation. At one point we came across a bunch of young kids who were playing where the creek flows into the lake. Right after we crossed a little girl cried out to us to help her brother who had drifted out and was franticly struggling to stay afloat and not drift out any farther. Mary knew how to swim and tried to rescue the kid, but she turned back realizing she wouldn't be able to pull it off. Meanwhile, I tried to call 9-1-1 but my crappy Tracfone had been damaged by the water and could only dial #-1-1.

Luckily for the kid though, a couple of older college guys had seen what was going on and one of them swam out and rescued the little bastard. Seeing that he was swimming out to save the kid, Mary and I went on our way up the beach not wanting to get involved. That, and we were both somewhat embarrassed by, but mostly ashamed of our inability to help.

I doubt I'll ever forget the image of Mary sitting on the beach all wet and looking like a goddess as the water dripped from her long red hair and her white tank top clung to her breasts leaving her midriff exposed as she smoked a cigarette and watched the waves. I wanted to push her down onto the sand and kiss her as our bodies writhed and the waves splashed against us just like that classic scene in From Here to Eternity.

After a cigarette or two we turned around and headed back to my house. Mary changed into some dry clothes and we hung out in my room for a little while. We played a game of chess, which she probably won, then sat on my bed watching TV for a little while. I took a couple pictures of us with the camera on my PDA. In both of them she was smiling for the camera while I stared into it looking incredibly unhappy. In reality, I was incredibly happy just to have her close to me and on my bed, but I had no energy to spare to smile as all of my being was dedicated to stopping myself from turning and kissing her. I hated myself for wanting to do it, but I hated myself for not doing it even more, and that was the emotion which shaped my expression.

To avoid any further temptation I got on my computer, which was completely separate from the TV back then. Glenn got a hold of us and came to pick us up. Not long after that everyone else showed up and the night went on like any other.

Back in those days, I had practically become Ferris and Mary's official third wheel. We hung out all the time whether anything was going on at Glenn's or not. Some other friends were around too, but I was a permanent fixture as if it had become a trio rather than a couple— aside from the fact that I wasn't gettin' any. I did everything I could just to see and be around Mary. To me, and only me, it was no longer Ferris and Mary it had become Mary! ... and? Oh yea... Ferris. Sure he was my friend and I liked the guy, but Glenn and I had been closer and better friends for much longer. Hanging out with Glenn though, did not ensure seeing Mary, but hanging out with Ferris did—so if I had the opportunity to choose, I got a hold of Ferris first almost every time.

Not too long after my worship of Mary had become well established and probably very obvious we had a chat online that made me die a little on the inside. She explained to me that things between Ferris and her had improved dramatically and that nothing was going to become of me and her. I told her, though I doubt she believed me, that I was crying and I really was—more than I can remember ever doing before or after that moment. I was in love with her, or at least as close to in love as I have been with anyone, and she knew it too. She told me not to say it. Grasping at straws I tried to get her to at least console me with the possibility that someday she and I might end up together. She wouldn't even lie and give me that though. She said she was sorry and wished she could do something to make me feel better. I told her if I could just get a hug from her from time to time it would help a lot, but she said even that would be impossible because she didn't want to screw things up with Ferris just when they'd finally gotten better. She hoped that our friendship wouldn't change and so did I but there's no way that was possible. After all, what the fuck kinda sham of a friendship can you have if you aren't even able to give your friend a hug when they really need one?

For a long ass time after that, I continued to hang out with Mary and Ferris a lot, but it was obvious that our friendship had been severely damaged. It was hard as fuck to see the two of them so happy and together. I could barely even look at her and when I did and she caught me there was no longer a smile shot her way but a depressed frown instead.

I wanted to hate her, but I couldn't; I still loved her way too much but I needed to hate someone, so I turned my hatred inward and placed it all on myself. I felt like less than a person for quite some time.

Wow!

I sound even more pathetic than I actually was.

It took a long time, but with a little denial I kinda recovered, if you can really call it that, by reverting back to how I had been beforehand, following Mary around like I was her little lamb every chance I got. I'd been going to concerts all the while with her, Ferris, and a group of people—even though I was never much of a music person. Don't get me wrong, I like to listen to it, but concerts were never really my thing and I don't know much music outside of Dylan, Sinatra, a cursory amount of classic rock, and an embarrassingly extensive number of gorgeous female singers whose music videos, (and in some cases just their voices themselves), I have jerked off to. It was still hard to be around Mary and Ferris, but it had gotten easier, and after awhile I even learned my place and stopped overstaying my welcome and worshiping Mary's every footstep.

At one of the concerts we went to I ran into this girl I went to high school with. Like everyone else that I went to high school with she knew I did a lot of drugs and smoked a lot of pot. I had cooled down my pot smoking considerably by this time though since I wasn't enjoying it that much anymore, but I still eagerly gave her my number when she suggested we get high together some time. My phone which had been on the fritz, because of the water damage from that day at the beach with Mary ended up breaking completely though. So, even if she wanted to get a hold of me she wouldn't have been able to.

I was pretty desperate to be with anyone to get Mary off my mind and in all honesty this girl seemed pretty easy and like a freak when it came to sex, so I invested some money into classmates.com to get her email address. I emailed her and within a week she responded giving me her phone number. We hung out quite a few times getting high and watching Comedy Central together or chillin' by the lake, but it wasn't very fun, especially because of the excessive amount of pot we were smoking. It quickly became clear to me that all we had in common was that we both got high and she wasn't really into me, just my weed. The only person she was into was her nephew whom she couldn't stop obsessing about since she'd had sex with him. I got fed up with it all pretty quickly.

One day I even covered the chair in my room that she usually sat in with laundry, so she'd have to sit next to me on the futon, but she just tossed the laundry aside without asking then sat down like usual and proceeded to ramble on about how amazing her nephew was and how much she wanted to be with him.

I literally got sick one week in the middle of winter and she called me once but I didn't answer. Soon after that, without any more minutes for my new Tracfone she would have had to have really wanted to get a hold of me and track me down at home. I've seen her a few times at the college since then, but I've taken evasive maneuvers to avoid having to talk to her.

Not long after Mary started going to college with us she met this douche bag musician that Ferris was friends with. He was so emo it was ridiculous, but he was a musician and Mary joined his band as the bass player so it pretty much goes without saying that she she ended up leaving Ferris for him.

Ferris was surprisingly cool about it, but Mary's close friends from school quickly turned on her calling her, "Whore," and, "Slut," all of them angry for Ferris, since he wasn't. She was surprised that the friends she'd met through Ferris were more accepting and understanding of the whole ordeal than the friends she'd made on her own. I think nearly everyone who knew them was at least a little shocked to see that the two people who represented the perfect couple to them had broken up, but her friends seemed way too invested in hating her because of it.

I resented the jackass that she'd left Ferris for. I knew first hand that she and Ferris were far from the perfect couple, but I couldn't help and wonder what was so great about this guy that was worth leaving Ferris for. More than that though, what bothered me was wondering what that cocksucking emo douche bag could have had that I didn't, well aside from a butt-plug engraved with his own initials of course. I suppose it was the whole musician thing since most girls tend to go for that.

She told me at one point that she first got into him, because he was very passionate and knowledgeable about both politics and music, and of course he was, "...soooo hot." She must've been a child molester in a past life in order to find that little faerie attractive.

Around that time I started hanging out with Ferris a lot more and going to IHOP with him. In part this was probably, because we'd run into Mary, sans the douche bag, now and then and I had no other means of seeing her on a regular basis, but doing so wasn't a conscious decision as it had been in the past.

It didn't take very long for the initial excitement of Mary's new relationship to wear off, and once that happened she started getting depressed all the time. I wonder, is being emo contagious? Maybe she caught it from him. After all, she did start cutting herself. If it is contagious we better shut down MySpace and Facebook and LiveJournal and a bunch of other websites, or we'll have an epidemic on our hands. It might already be too late though. I only hope that these idiots start actually bleeding to death instead of just covering themselves with scars, maybe we can get some heroin addicts to help them actually find a vein.

Anyhow, in those days Mary and I hung out a few times, and in my infinite stupidity and hopeless romanticism I fell for her all over again—honestly thinking I had a real shot with her. She told me that emo boy had lost his passion for everything: politics, music, life, and more than anything else her. I figured that if it was someone with passion for her that she wanted it was obvious that I was the perfect man for the job.

One day, not long after the car accident I was in with my dad, riding a sort of post-accident-gotta-live-life-without-any-regrets high I wrote a poem to her. I made it into a little book with a blue folder cut to size to form the front and back covers.

Chapter 17.5.5

Appendix B: Part II

One day at IHOP while I was sitting and talking with Mary, I read over the blue book poem to make sure it was satisfactory. Truthfully, I just wanted her to inquire as to what it was and after awhile she did. I told her, "It's something I wrote for and want to give someone I like, but I'm debating if I should do that or just destroy it."

"You should just give it to 'em ... whatcha have to lose?" she asked.

"You're right, I will."

"You shouldn't listen to me though, I don't know much when it comes to relationships; look at the one I'm in now."

"Yea, I think I'll go with your original advice though."

A cigarette or two later I was looking through her sketchbook and after a little while, making sure she saw, I slipped the poem in the back. She got a scared look on her face as if she was thinking, 'Oh shit! It was for me! How didn't I see that coming? And why the hell did I tell him to just go for it?'

She gave it back to me trying to make sure no one else saw her do so.

Once I'd put it away she quietly said, "I'm sorry, I didn't know it was for me, I can't accept it."

"You don't even wanna read it?"

"No, I have a good idea of what it says already... sorry."

It was awkward the rest of that night, but things returned to normal the next day. I bet she was expecting me to look even more depressed than her boyfriend when she saw me at school, because she looked surprised when I showed up more chipper and energetic than usual. 'At least I tried!' was my unspoken mantra.

I did get her to read it later though, actually it was on the day that she broke up with that douche bag. We hung out and she read some of the poems I'd written for a poetry class and when this was the only poem of mine she hadn't read her curiosity got the best of her. We were sitting at IHOP again when she read the following.

*(Initially I had intended for this
to be a blank solid blue page,
but due to obvious costing issues
you will have to use your imagination.)*

<u>A Poem Just For
You</u>

written by
Alden Baird
for
Mary
(a good friend, muse,
and the most beautiful person I've ever met)

<u>The author's rambling disclaimer</u>!

READ BEFORE TURNING THE PAGE

1) If I'm going too far with this it's only
   because I have spent so much time
   not going far enough.
2) Please don't get weird on me after
   reading this, unless it is a good
   kind of weird.
3) As implied by the title don't
   show this to anyone else.
4) See point 2 but read the
   the first word three times.
5) Though it is not necessary some
   form of response would be
   much appreciated.
6) Finally, this is the only copy of this
   manuscript in existence aside from
   a very rough draft of the poem.
   As was with my previous work
   analyzing the length of your hair
   I leave its fate in your hands alone.
7) Ahh, hell. See points 2 and 4 one last
   time for good measure

I realized the other day,
That you've never heard me say
"I love you."
For that I am sorry.
But know that I love you deeply,
Know that I have cried for hours
As I tried to make that feeling go away
So that I could be happy for you
While you were happy with
My friend,
Your boyfriend,
Who is now only a mutual friend.

Even in my dreams
You are the girl of my dreams.
Yet in all the time I've spent
Writing poems about you,
Trying to capture
How you make me feel.
I have committed a horrible atrocity,
I have never written your name,
For which I am also sorry.

Your name that continues to march
    through my mind
Without fatigue
From the ongoing marathon in my thoughts
That it began over two years ago
But now I will.
No!
Now I must!
Let it free on this page for a moment.

So it can see how much
I love you and in turn love it.
And so it may leave its permanent impression here.
So you will know
That I am overflowing with love for you.

Mary
4 letters
that combine to make my heart flutter,
Mary
2 syllables
that make me weak in the knees
Mary
1 word that always makes me smile,
Mary
Yes you!
Mary
the girl I love.

So when you do hear me say, "I love you."
I hope you'll say, "I love you too."

*(Initially I had intended for this
to be a blank solid blue page,
but due to obvious costing issues
you will have to use your imagination.)*

God! I find it hard to believe after reading this poem that I actually expected to win her over with it. Sure it's sweet, but if being sweet was going to win her over she would have left Ferris for me back in the days of his Diablo 2 obsession—despite the fact that she was dependent on him to buy her things and pay for her concert tickets, drugs, and food. Besides, more than anything else it seems to me to be incredibly pathetic in retrospect.

Love poems aren't the way to get girls in this day and age though.

Sure they work to make a girl that's already into you feel giddy and happy knowing how much you care about her and that you're thinking about her when she's not around, more than any amount of flowers or chocolates or electric basses and guitars for gifts, but she has to be into you in the first place—otherwise all your efforts are just futile and embarrassing.

Not that you shouldn't keep with that 'At least I tried!' attitude, but the key word to that is tried; at some point you have to stop fucking trying.

There's gotta be at least one hopelessly romantic girl out there though, someone who'd melt over shit like this, but chances are she's going out with some asshole that doesn't appreciate her and makes her feel so inferior that she's happy she's been blessed enough to be with him.

Chapter 17 (Cont'd) (Cont'd)

Mary (Just Mary)

As she finished reading it, Mary saw Ferris pull up in his car and hastily slid the poem across the table to give it back to me. She smiled as she said, "That one's my favorite."

"It's yours if you want it."

"I wouldn't know what to do with it."

That's all the response I ever got.

Maybe I should have learned to play guitar and wrote a song instead, that probably would have had a better chance to win her over than any amount of written words expressing my love for her.

But then again, I probably only have myself to blame. If in the very beginning I had the balls and follow through to actually act on my feelings and not just write about them things might have gone a lot differently.

How's the saying go?

Actions speak louder than words.

Well, I have always been a very soft spoken person.

Anyways, shortly after that I left town for two weeks to visit my brother in Florida, and by the time I got back

Mary and Ferris were all but officially back together. A week after I'd gotten back the three of us went to Bonnaroo together. Independent of each other they had both practically begged me to go with them while Mary was still going out with the emo douche. They didn't want it to be awkward, ex-boyfriend and girlfriend spending three whole days together, and Mary figured that her shitty ass boyfriend would be cooler with it if there was someone else going with them.

Since a dramatic change of circumstances had obviously occurred I had once again become their out of place third wheel. The first night, I had a sorta freak out brought on by the stress of the whole situation, and the fact that I hadn't slept since waking up to pack for the trip at noon the previous day.

I was in the screen tent just chillin' while they took a nap together on their air mattress in the sleeping tent. I heard them talking about how it would be better if I wasn't there and Mary told him she didn't want to be with me. That this actually happened was denied that night, making me think I really was losing it, but some of it was confirmed later—though it was still sloppily coated in sugar by a drunken Ferris.

Anyhow, thinking they were just fake sleeping while I went into the tent to grab a notebook I sang a little tune, to myself. It went something like this, "*If you don't want someone 'round. You should just, tell 'em to their face. It'd make things a lot, easier. For ev'ry one involved.*"

I wrote for a little bit then went back into the tent and laid down on the cot. Still awake, Ferris asked me, "Tryin' to get some sleep?"

"Yea, doubt I'll be able to though."

"Yea."

After some time spent trying to get some shut eye I asked Ferris, "You awake?"

"Yea."

"Can I get an honest answer if I ask you a question?"

"Yea."

"Would you rather I have not come here with you guys?"

"No man."

I thought for a minute, debating whether or not to leave them alone for a little while after making some sort of dramatic exit that would render them incapable of enjoying the time I'd given them.

"I'm gonna give you two some time alone." I told him.

"Why?"

I answered him angrily saying, "Because I'm positive you were lying through your teeth just now." I started getting out of the tent and before he could utter a word of protest I zipped it shut saying, "I'll be back in an hour."

I explored the campgrounds and returned to our site an hour later. They were getting ready to check out one of the opening night shows and try to find me if I didn't return. However, I'm skeptical that there's any truth in that second part. Between their lies I profusely apologized to them and from there on the rest of the trip went a lot better.

We all ended up taking acid and ecstasy the next day and had a blast. Hearing Dave Matthews play from our tent was sort of a buzzkill, but we were still so gone when his set ended that we went to the concert area through the exit instead of the entrance and had to wade through a sea of Dave's fans. When we made it through the crowd we realized that somehow we had not passed the security check point, so we ended up having to go in the right way anyway.

I was still the third wheel and we'd always part ways when they went shopping or I went out to get drugs, but I had a better time than I did at the previous Bonnaroo. The weather was better, the people I didn't care for weren't there, and despite the general weirdness between the three of us—I at least had a blast.

The one time they had me lead the way out of the crowd of a concert pissed me off though. They quickly became impatient and found their own way out. When I caught up to them Mary told me, "You should never be a leader."

I said, "Yea." but I was thinking, 'Listen bitch, just because you two couldn't wait five seconds for someone to move doesn't necessarily make me a bad leader, you just suck balls as followers.'

Anyway, they didn't enjoy our time there nearly as much as I did. The selection of bands wasn't as good as the previous year and they had me tagging along just as they were beginning to rekindle their relationship. On the final day we ended up leaving early instead of staying the night and leaving the next morning like we'd done the previous year.

After Bonnaroo, they officially got back together, but when the next semester of school came around Mary left Ferris for a different musician that once again she'd met through him. This one seems much cooler than the first and I think they're still together, despite the fact that they've temporarily broken up once or twice.

I haven't seen her much since then though; we hung out a few times when she needed help moving into the apartment she had for about six months and again when she needed help paying the rent and I had the money to spare. Now, she lives with her dad in northern Illinois and as far as I know barely anyone sees her anymore. Often when I do see her these days I get the distinct feeling, impression, and/or vibe that she doesn't really even like me as a person anymore—let alone have any remaining romantic feelings for me. I have ceased to care about what she thinks of me though or at least that's what I tell myself. I wasted way too much time pursuing her. I feel like I was an overly persistent Steve Urkel at times, albeit not nearly as nerdy and a shit load less annoying, but then again I didn't experience my obsessive love from her end. I probably have been pretty damn frustrating and annoying to her.

On my twenty first birthday, I got wasted as shit at the bar and told Ferris, "I loved Mary more than you ever did."

He got kinda angry at that statement, but took it in stride since I was drunk as shit and it was both my twenty-first and golden birthday. That's probably not even in the top 5 worst things I did that night though, but that's an entirely different story which I remember very little of first hand, as should be the case with twenty-first birthdays. I refuse however to ever take back that statement. I've apologized for it, but only because I'm truly sorry that it's true.

Chapter 18

Catching Up is Small-talk

"Alden."

...

"Alden."

...

"Alden!"

...

"ALDEN!"

I jump up exclaiming, "Huh?!... What?!" as I look around the family room, disorientated.

Glenn and Neil both look at me laughing. Glenn holds up the tequila bottle saying, "Don't go falling asleep on me, there's still more drinkin' to do."

I take off my glasses and rub my face with both hands saying, "I wasn't asleep, I was just lost in... in..." I look up and shake it off before finishing, "...in thought."

Neil says, "Jeez you weren't kidding about getting too high."

I nod and say, "Yea." then light a cigarette.

Glenn pours a couple shots then get up holding one out to me. He says, "What better to counter act the pot than a shot?"

I grab the shot glass taking care not to spill it as I say, "I can think of quite a few things, but I guess this'll have to do."

We raise our shot glasses and Glenn says, "Cheers." Before we both slam them down.

Glenn sits down and a moment later we all hear a car door slam shut. Glenn looks over at me saying, "I wonder if that's Mary."

I say, "Most likely." Then, hearing a knock on the window only a matter of seconds later I immediately jump up saying, "I'll get it."

Glenn says, "Okay," and leans back on the couch as I quickly make my way to the front door.

Somehow, I'm still controlled by the force of my old habit to rush and open the door in order to see Mary before anyone else.

I open the door and Mary is on the other side. She's still got the same red hair, though she's taken a curling iron to it and it looks like she traded in her hippie-chick look for a slightly different, but equally attractive farmer's daughter style. Maybe it's just the cowboy hat though.

She says, "Hi." and I say, "Hey!" as I turn around and head back towards the family room.

Closing the door she asks, "How's it goin'?"

I turn back to respond, "I'm alright, you?"

"Meh, alright I guess."

Why is it that she always says she's alright while making sure to express the fact that she isn't alright at all?

She heads towards the kitchen and I go back into the family room.

Not seeing anyone behind me, Glenn asks, "Who was it?"

I sit down and say, "It's Mary, I think she's grabbing something to drink."

"Cool."

As Mary makes her way toward the room Glenn turns and greets her with a loud, "Heeeey!"

She says, "Hi," as she comes in.

Neil actually turns his attention completely away from the computer for the first time since we left Glenn's room. He greets Mary saying, "Heeey, it's been awhile."

As she sits down in the chair closest to Glenn she says, "Yea, it's been too long." We all light a cigarette and turn our attention toward her. She follows our lead and lights up one of her own.

Glenn asks, "So, what've you been up to?"

"Not too much."

Neil asks, "You still working at that news station?"

"Nah, I haven't been workin' there for awhile."

"Really?"

"Yea it's been like, six months or so."

"Damn, it really has been a long time."

"Yea, I'm working at Applebee's now."

"How's that?"

"Meh, it's alright."

I chime in, "As long as it pays, right?"

She shrugs saying, "I guess," then asks, "You working yet Alden?"

I laugh and say, "Well, I start back at the tax office pretty soon, but that aside no jobs for me."

Belittling me she says, "You should just go out and get a job instead of just waiting for that."

"Eh, jobs aren't my thing. I'm gonna work as little as I possibly can as long as I can get away with it."

She shakes her head and shoots me a look that says, 'You're still just the same old loser you've always been, get off your lazy ass and join the real world.'

Fuck the so called "real" world!
People always act like their way of life is the only right way to live, whether they're talking about religious beliefs or just their day to day routine. We're all in the fucking real world people! We were born into it for fuck's sake. It doesn't become real only once we've graduated high school or college or once we've gotten a job.

Attempting to defend myself I say, "Hey, I had a couple job interviews at the library. I don't interview very well though."

Chuckling, Glenn asks me, "What was that one answer you gave them?"

"Oh... They asked something along the lines of, 'How would you treat old people and children?' and I replied, 'Well, for starters, I wouldn't treat old people like children.'"

Glenn laughs and Mary and Neil both shake their heads. Still laughing, Glenn says, "That's a great answer."

"Well, the two are very different." Neil says after some thought.

Agreeing I say, "Yea," then looking over at Mary I add, "That's the first thing that came to mind, I elaborated, but it was two elderly women that interviewed me so I don't think they appreciated that sorta smart ass answer," I stand up and walk over by Glenn adding, "and that's only the funniest example of me putting my foot in my mouth."

I grab the bottle of tequila and poor myself a shot.

Glenn grabs the bottle from me as I set it down. "I'll have one too!" he exclaims and he pours himself a shot that overflows and gets tequila all over the table.

Everyone laughs as he exclaims, "Shit!"

"Nice one," I say.

Mary says, "Smoooooth."

Glenn gets up and leaves the room muttering, "God damn it, mother fucker."

He quickly returns with a wad of paper towels in his hands and angrily wipes up the spill. Throwing the now tequila flavored paper towels into the garbage can he asks Mary, "You want a shot?"

She answers, "No," making a face similar to the one she'd have made if she had actually taken a shot.

"Neil?" he asks.

I ask Glenn, "Why are you even still tryin'?"

Neil says, "My thoughts exactly."

Glenn ignores us and asks him again, "So, you takin' a shot with us?"

Neil exclaims, "No! And quit fucking asking!" then angrily turns his attention to the computer again.

Glenn says, "Jeez, alright man." then he turns to Mary and asks, "You sure you don't want a shot?"

Shaking her head she says, "Nope."

"Come on, you're twenty-one now, you should drink."

"Not hapnin'"

"Come on, even Neil at least took one."

"No, I ..."

Glenn cuts her off saying, "Hey Neil, you took a shot with us. Tell Mary."

Neil turns to Glenn asking, "What?! What the fuck are you talking about now?"

"You took a shot with us right?"

"I'm not taking a shot damnit!"

Mary and I both laugh.

"That's not what I asked!"

Before they get in a battle between the drunk and the annoyed I slowly say, "He asked if you took a shot, not if you would take one." enunciating every syllable.

"Oh," Neil responds, "Yea, you know I took one. Why the hell'd you ask?"

Looking at Mary and pointing at Neil, Glenn exclaims, "See!"

"Don't do it Mary, that shit is horrible. Glenn likes it because he's an alcoholic and Alden, well, he's just fuckin' crazy."

Mary laughs and I tell Glenn, "Come on let's just do these shots, we gotta drink to that one."

He looks at me then back at Mary saying, "Come on."

"Nope."

He turns back to me and says, "Alright, fuck these guys, let's do this."

We both take our shot and I sit back down.

Glenn asks Mary, "Why aren't ya drinkin'?"

She answers, "It's not that I won't drink, I just don't like tequila. I could go for a beer if you have any."

Excited, Glenn says, "I think we have some," then asks, "any pref'rence?"

"No, surprise me."

I check to see if I finished my soda as Glenn stands up.

It's empty, and beer will probly go much better with tequila anyways.

"Grab me one too." I tell him.

"You care what kind it is?"

"No, as long as it's not Jaguar."

Glenn laughs and Mary asks, "What's that?"

He tells her, "It's some really strong beer that comes in a big can so each one is like drinking three or so beers."

"And it tastes nasty as shit too," I add.

Mary cringes and Glenn tells her, "Alden had three once and had a horrible hang over, but don't worry we don't have any."

"Good."

Glenn asks, "Neil, you want a beer?"

Turning around Neil says, "Sure, whatcha got?"

"Not sure."

"Okay, I'll go with you."

"Works for me."

Neil hops up out of his chair and follows Glenn out of the room. Mary and I give each other a few awkward glances.

We barely ever talk anymore and whenever we do see each other we never know what to say, so we usually end up sitting and suffering through an awkward silence. We're not really part of each others' lives anymore and whenever I see her it just reminds me of how stupid I was in regards to her in the past. Part of me still wants her just as much as I did back then which makes me feel even stupider since I should know better than that by now. That, and I have been trying to convince myself for quite some time that love or any emotion even remotely close to it is total bullshit, and an illusion brought on by much baser things. Whenever I see her though feelings start to rise to the surface that shatter the shell of cynical reasoning that I surround myself with.

I light a cigarette and break the awkward silence asking, "So how are you and your boyfriend doing?"

Of course I jump right into the status of her current relationship. What else could we possibly talk about?

She lights a smoke and answers, "He has a name you know."

I want to say I don't care enough about the guy to refer to him by his name, but instead I just say, "Sorry, I forget what it was."

She looks at me skeptically knowing that I have always taken enough interest in her love life to not forget her boyfriend's name, "It's Kyle."

I try to fake like I didn't remember it all along saying, "Oh yeah, Kyle... Kyle." as if hearing it aloud made it suddenly click.

I can tell by the look on her face that she's not really buying it though.

You've never been a good liar.
I know.

"Anyhow," I continue, "How are things on that front?"

"Meh, alright, we don't get to see each other too much, but it's great when we do."

"That's cool... didn't you guys break up for awhile?"

"Yea, not for very long though."

"Cool, cool."

"You get yourself a girlfriend yet?"

I laugh and say, "I'll give you two guesses and one of 'em doesn't count."

"I'll take that as a no."

"Of course it's a no, you know me."

What the hell did I even mean by that?

We both turn toward the door as Glenn and Neil come back in. As he enters, Glenn says, "Alright, Neil got the last Spotted Cow. I got High Life for the rest of us though."

I say, "Cool, thanks," as he hands me one.

Neil cracks his beer open and reclaims the computer chair. Glenn hands Mary her beer and she says, "Danka." Mary opens her beer and as he sits down Glenn pulls another beer out of his pocket like some sorta magic trick. He and I both crack our beers open simultaneously then look at each other.

"That was weird." I say.

Chapter 19

Belligerence and Blah Blah Blah

We all sit around drinking our beers for a little while as we watch a bunch of random comedians on TV who range from halfway decent to incredibly horrible. After awhile Neil looks up at the clock and groans, "I gotta get goin' pretty soon."

Glenn says, "What?! Don't be a little bitch and go home so early."

Everyone laughs except Neil who says, "Hey! I have to work at nine in the morning."

"So what? I have to work at eleven and I'm drinkin'."

"I don't want to go in all tired and hung over though."

"Pussy!"

I add my two cents, "Glenn doesn't go in hung over and tired, he's still drunk as shit when he gets to work."

Glenn exclaims, "Hell yeah, that deserves a shot!"

He starts pouring one up as Neil says, "Unlike you Glenn, I'd actually like to keep my job."

"Why the fuck would you wanna keep working in that fuckin' hell hole?"

Neil answers him, "I actually..."

He is cut short as Mary asks, "What hell hole?"

Glenn answers, "Quizno's!"

Surprised, she asks Neil, "You still work there?"

He answers, "Yea," then continues with what he was telling Glenn, "I actually like working there."

Glenn holds up his index finger giving Neil the international signal for 'Hold on.' and says, "Hold that thought, man."

"O-kay."

Turning to me Glenn says, "Get over here Alden we're doing this shot."

"You're on your own for that one."

"Oh no," he says while filling a second shot glass, "you're taking this one with me, it's already poured."

As I get up and walk across the room I say, "Alright, I'll take the fucking shot."

"That's what I like to hear."

I light a cigarette and we both take a shot. I tell him, "Next time you try that shit you're gonna be doin' two shots by yourself."

"Fair enough."

Neil rolls his eyes and asks, "You done now?"

Glenn grabs the bottle, holds it up, and says, "Fuck no! There's still plenty to drink."

Mary laughs.

"Not that! You told me to hold that thought. So can we get this over with now?"

"Oh." He thinks for a moment then asks, "What was the last thing you said?"

Trying to remember, Neil mutters, "Um, Ahh. Hmm."

I say, "Neil had just said that he actually..."

Mary cuts me off getting straight to the point, "He likes working at Quizno's."

"Yea," Neil agrees then looking at Glenn he adds, "and you told me to hold that thought so you guys could take that shot."

Glenn stares at him, looking completely dumbfounded, trying to think of what he was going to say before that all important shot had broken his train of thought.

Don't you hate when that happens?

It happens to me all the fucking time. Usually it's either something vital or important and relevant to the conversation at hand, or it at least feels that way when you have no memory of what it was you were going to say, so if you don't manage to recall what it was it bothers you all day long.

You can't stop thinking, "What the fuck? What the fuck was it? God damn it! I know it had something to do with... What the fuck? What the fuck was it? God damn it! I know it had something to do with... What the fuck? What the fuck was it? God damn it! I know it had something to do with... What the fuck? What the fuck was it? God damn it! I know it had something to do with..." until something else manages to take and hold your attention long enough for you to forget there was something that you forgot.

If however, something triggers the memory that you forgot something, you will be back where you started or worse; you might not even remember the context around which you forgot it, so you'll no longer even have that valuable point of reference. When you remember, if it ever happens, it usually turns out to be something really stupid but it's definitely nothing that was so witty or brilliant that it forever improves the lives of everyone blessed enough to hear it.

Now where the fuck were we?
I know Glenn was...
Oh yeah.

Remembering what he was going to say, Glenn asks Neil, "Are you fucking retarded?"

Mary and I both burst into laughter as a shocked Neil asks, "What?!"

Glenn says, "Wait! Hear me out!" quieting us down before he asks Neil, "How the fuck can you like working there with those fuckin' towel-heads?"

"I don't know."

"I hated that fuckin' place; fuckin' guy buys it and takes over, havin' his own family work and order us around. Fuck that!"

Neil looks at both Mary and me then asks, "I'm sure Glenn has told you both some crazy ass horror stories about working at Quizno's, right?"

"Oh yeah!" I answer.

Mary nods in agreement and Neil continues, "Glenn makes it out to be a lot worse than it actually is. He exaggerates that shit a lot."

Glenn yells out, "Bullshit!"

"No! If you would've just done your job, not gone in fucking trashed, and acted professional at work it would've been fine."

"No, that place fuckin' sucked ass, and what the fuck are you talking about? 'Do my job, act professional,' I busted my ass at that place for years before I finally got fed up with their bullshit and quit."

"You do know they were gonna fire you?"

"Yeah, sure."

"No, seriously, they were plannin' on firing you for being trashed half the time and saying all sorts of vulgar shit in front of the customers."

Glenn admits, "Well, I did do that a lot... but fuck the people that came into Quizno's they were all retards and assholes!"

Neil tells him, "You're gonna have to deal with that regardless of where you work."

Mary agrees saying, "Yea, pretty much everywhere I've worked I've had to deal with a lot of idiots and assholes, especially when it comes to dealing with customers."

Glenn concedes, "I'll give you that..." before adding, "but still, it doesn't matter because I quit."

"They were about to fire you though!" Neil persists.

"That doesn't matter, I quit before they could do it."

"Whatever."

I tell Glenn, "You should've just waited till they fired you and been able to collect unemployment."

Laughing, Neil agrees, "Yea, you should've."

Glenn exclaims, "Shit!" no longer contesting that he was going to get fired, "I never thought of that."

I add, "When you work at a place as long as you worked there I think it looks pretty good on your resume, regardless of whether or not you're fired."

"Yea."

Mary corrects me saying, "I think it depends on why you got fired though."

"Yea," I say, "but unless it's for something really bad, like stealing from them or embezzling money it's gotta look relatively good."

"I suppose." she says.

Neil points out, "Coming to work drunk all the time and scaring off all the customers is pretty damn bad though."

"Yea, you're right about that." I say.

You know every time I've hung out with Glenn and Neil since Glenn quit that job they've gotten into this argument like it's some sort of comedy routine. Shit, they've probably been having the same argument about whether or not Quizno's was a shitty place to work at, minus the bit about the firing, since shortly after the Neil first got him the job.

Glenn asks, "Can we get back to the point? We know I hated Quizno's and all that, but how the hell can you like working there?"

Neil thinks for a second, then answers, "I don't really know, I suppose I'm just used to it so it comes easily, and I'd rather not have to start somewhere else and get comfortable with a job all over again."

"I guess I can understand that."

Suddenly, Nina pokes her head in the door and says, "Hi, everybody."

Neil says, "Hi."

I say, "Hey, Nina."

Mary says, "Hi."

And Glenn says, "Hey."

She awkwardly looks at us for a minute, since we are all just staring at her expecting her to say something. Finally, she says, "Alllllright, I just wanted to say, 'Hi.' I'm gonna go take a shower now."

"Later."

"Later."

She closes the door and heads down the hallway.

Changing the subject from Quizno's, Neil asks Mary, "So, you still living with that one girl?"

Mary laughs and says, "Wow you really are outta the loop. I've been living down in Illinois for practically two years now."

"Jeez. How did I not know that? No one tells me anything anymore."

Having not paid a bit of attention to the conversation since he was preparing and taking a shot, Glenn says, "What's this about Illinois? Fucking FIBs."

In Wisconsin, especially the area near Illinois and even more specifically near Chicago, we often refer to people from Illinois as FIBs. This stands for Fucking Illinois Bastard or Fucking Illinois Bastards in this case, hence the lower case s.

Sorry, you're not retarded, I shouldn't have had to explain how acronyms work to you, but that little prick at the bookstore and/or the asshole that you borrowed this book from... well, let's just say they're a little slow.

Anyhow, being from Illinois and now once again a resident of that shitty state Mary exclaims, "Hey! Fuck you too, Glenn."

Glenn turns to her and says, "Oh shit! I forgot you're from Illinois, aren't you?"

"Yea, and I'm living there now too!"

"Oh yeah, you living with your dad still?"

"Yup."

"I'm sorry. You know I love you Mary."

"Yea. I love you too, Glenn."

Hearing that Neil and I both put our heads down in mock depression.

She turns to Neil and says, "You know I love you too Neil."

He shyly smiles and raises his arms in a sort of victory pose for a second. I light a cigarette, and Mary and I both exchange an awkward glance.

She won't say it to me.

She never has, whether it be over the impersonal internet or just something like this where, "I love you." doesn't really mean that, it means something more like, "I enjoy your company," or, "I value your friendship." There have been times that she has gone around a whole room of people—whether she be drunk, stoned, tripping, or even plain sober—and told everyone that she loved them except me. She'll just skip over me altogether or stop dead in her tracks and change the subject once she gets to me.

I've always wondered why she's done this without fail over the years. Maybe she thinks that I'll take it literally and it will jump-start a whole new round of me trying to hook up with her. Hell, if I knew for sure she meant it that way it probably would, but by now it'd take so much fucking convincing that she'd be the one chasing after me for once.

It could be that she doesn't say it because she really does have feelings for me and feels uncomfortable vocalizing them in front of everyone, and/or cheapening them by playing it off as if what she means is one of those simple "You're a good friend!" type statements. I have

however trained myself to not even consider ideas like that
as possibilities beyond a wet dream of a fantasy. It's
probably just something as simple as the fact that she
doesn't enjoy my company, or consider me to be a good
friend at all.

Well, fuck her anyways!

Mary's phone rings and she answers it excitedly, "Hi!
... Good, you? ... That's good. ... I'm over at Glenn's. ...
Glenn's! ... GLENN'S!! ... Hangin' out with Glenn, Neil,
and Alden ... Neil and Alden! ... Yea. ... You wanna come
over here and hang out for a lil' bit? ... Oh, alright. ... I'll
be there shortly. ... Love ya. ... Bye."

Glenn looks at her and asks, "What's up?"

"I'm meeting up with Kyle at I-HOP."

"I see how it is, you and him are too good for us so
you're gonna go hang out with all your cool new friends."

"No, it's not that, he just had plans to meet some
people out there."

Sure, he just doesn't care for us. He's Mr. Cool-
musician-that-has-his-life-together guy and were just a
bunch of fuckin' losers that never grew out of the lazy,
video game playing, getting fucked up stage of our lives.

"Suuure." Glenn says in an exaggerated fashion.

"No, seriously."

"Yea, yea, yea."

Mary finishes her beer and stands up. She goes up to
Glenn and they do our group's hand shake. It's a pretty
simple handshake; the only original thing about it is that it
ends with each person miming hitting a joint and ditching

the roach to their left, though even that is probably not very original at all when I really think about it.

She says. "Seeya Glenn."

"Seeya."

She walks over to Neil and says, "It was good seeing you again."

"Yea, it's been too long."

They do a regular hand shake followed by a fist bump since Neil never learned the other one, because he wasn't around when it was the happenin' thing to do.

"I'll see you," he says, "and hopefully soon this time."

"Yea, gimme a call, we'll work something out."

"Okay, you need to hear some of my new music."

"You're making music again?!"

"Yea, mostly collaborating over the internet though, since no one in the old band lives around here."

"That's still cool."

They talk for a moment about their old band which consisted of Mary, Neil, and few other guys. I tune most of it out since I don't understand what the fuck they're talkin' about and I am preoccupied by going over various ways to say, "Goodbye." to her in my head.

"Seeya."?

Too simple, and Glenn said it already.

"Good seeing you."?

Neil is pretty much playing out the rest of that conversation.

"Later, sexy."?

Definitely not my style. Why'd I even think that? Must be one of those phrases that people overused in high school so much that it got trapped in my subconscious.

Eh, I'll just go with old reliable.

Wait, why the fuck am I thinking about this like it fuckin' matters?

Having finished talking to Neil, Mary approaches me and says, "I'll seeya Alden."

As we do the whole handshake thing I look up at her, smile, and say, "Seeya, Mary."

She smiles then turns to leave the room. Glenn tells her, "Get the fuck outta here, we don't need you."

Mary laughs as she walks down the hall and before she turns the corner Glenn yells out, "And next time wear a fuckin' low cut shirt!"

We all laugh; even Neil can't cut it short and disapprovingly shake his head like earlier. Mary grins and proceeds to leave.

After hearing the front door close, Neil tells Glenn, "I can't believe you actually said that to her."

"Really? I thought that it was something very me of me to say."

"I guess you're right."

Changing the subject, Glenn asks, "So, Alden, shot?"

I stand up saying, "Yea, why not?"

He pours up the shots and we slam them down. I light a cigarette and sit back down. Neil snags the chair Mary was using, but immediately gets back up to snag his beer from the computer desk.

Chapter 20

An Abrupt End to a Bottle of Tequila

Glenn, Neil, and I all watch TV for a little while without saying a word. The whole time, Neil constantly shakes his beer can to check how much of it is left. I only notice this, because I periodically look over at him thinking that I should have snagged that seat in order to sit in and catch even a small whiff of Mary's scent.

For some reason, whenever I see Mary I can't get her out of my mind for awhile afterwards. I've worked it down to a maximum of two days, making it like a twenty-four or forty-eight hour love, or maybe just lust, sickness that she always gives me. Among the symptoms are the inability to get her out of my head, the feeling of being a total idiot, a mild amount of shame, a significantly larger amount of disgust with myself, and the inability to get off to the thought of almost anyone except her—the only exceptions being whoever happens to be in the top three of my hottest women in the world list at the time, but sometimes I'll still groan out her name when I cum. Without putting a significant amount of effort towards numbing my mind I have a feeling that is going to be case tonight, but that might be avoided as without any real thought or consideration, one of the more self-destructive symptoms seems to have come to the surface, because...

 I suddenly find myself standing on the other side of the room with the tequila bottle in hand practically touching my lips.

Glenn looks up at me asking, "What the hell are you doing?!"

I look at the tequila bottle then him. Shrugging, I ask, "Shot?"

He nods and I pour one up for each of us. We slam them down and I light a smoke before pouring myself another shot and taking it.

As I start to pour myself a third shot, Glenn snags the bottle from me and pours himself one. Seeing all this and having finished his beer Neil gets up and starts putting his jacket on.

Glenn turns to him and asks, "What's going on?"

Neil says, "I gotta work in the morning and..." he trails off to avoid saying that he doesn't want to get stuck taking care of two drunk people, or have any part in the insanity he imagines is about to unfold with Glenn and myself on the verge of entering an unofficial drinking contest.

As Neil and Glenn do the whole handshake fist bump thing, Glenn says, "Alright, you pussy. Seeya."

Neil tells him, "Seeya." then approaches me. I try to do the other handshake with him, but we both end up wiggling our hands around like retards and laughing as he says, "I don't know that one."

Still laughing, I say, "Seeya man."

"Seeya."

He grabs his Wii and heads out.

Hearing the front door slam shut Glenn says, "I bet he forgot his keys or somethin'."

I slam my shot then say, "I wouldn't doubt it."

Glenn quickly takes his shot and grabs the bottle before I can get my hands on it. He says, "Yea."

He goes to pour himself another shot and I give him a look that says, 'Your better pour me one up too.' He smirks, but before he can start pouring we hear a knock on the window.

Glenn exclaims, "I fucking called it!" while jumping up out of his seat.

"Yea, ya did."

Glenn sets the bottle on the table and goes to let Neil back in. I take the liberty of pouring up the next round myself. Neil walks in and seeing me pouring shots he shakes his head before starting to look around where he was sitting.

I ask him, "What'd you forget?"

"My fucking keys." he answers.

Glenn comes back in asking, "Didn't I fuckin' call it?"

I tell Neil, "Yea, he even got what it was right."

Neil finds his keys by the computer and checks his pockets a few times.

"Got everything?" Glenn asks.

He answers, "I hope so." then heads out of the room saying, "Seeya guys."

We both say, "Seeya man." and Neil leaves. This time he doesn't have to come back for anything.

With Neil gone I point to the shots and Glenn nods. We both take one and Glenn asks, "So... why the sudden burst of drinkin'?"

I shrug to avoid explaining something I am not even entirely sure of then say, "Just get the urge to get fucked up and forget things sometimes, and given the circumstances drinking seems like the best course of action. You know the feeling."

Glenn knowingly smiles as he grabs the bottle right out from under my hands and pours up another round of shots. Picking up his, he asks, "She really gets to you doesn't she?"

I grab my shot and slam it before saying, "More than I would like to admit."

"You know I was kinda hurt back in the day when you started hanging out with her and Ferris and stopped coming over here all the time, but more and more I think I get it."

"Well, it was really nothing against you, it was just... I wanted to be able to see her, and at the time that was the only way I could be sure it would happen."

"Yea," he says, "I realize that now."

As Glenn pours up yet another round of shots, Nina comes into the room and looks around. Surprised to only see the two of us, she asks, "Where the fuck did everyone go?"

Glenn answers, "Neil just left since it's past his bed time or some shit, and Mary left a little while ago to go to I-HOP."

Nina snags the computer chair saying, "That's shitty."

Glenn raises his shot to me as he says, "Yea, they weren't drinking though, so fuck 'em."

We take our shots as Nina laughs and hops on the computer. I get away from the bottle for a moment to let that last wave of shots kick in and take my seat again.

Larry the Cable Guy or one of those other annoying blue collar comedians, not Ron White though, (even at his worst he is a least tolerable), comes on TV. Glenn sighs, turns to the TV Guide channel, mutes the TV, and asks Nina, "Hey, can you play some music while you're on there?"

She turns toward him asking, "Huh?"

"Play some music!"

"Oh, okay, just gimme a minute."

"No, do it now! You can do whatever the hell you're doing as it plays."

She turns to me and asks, "How much have you guys been drinking?!"

"Oh, I probably should've warned you, quite a lot over the last 15 minutes or so."

Glenn asks her, "What makes you think we're drunk?"

She turns her attention back to the computer saying, "Probably the fact that you're acting like a total ass."

"Harsh," I say.

Glenn brushes it off like she never said a thing and asks, "So, Nina, you want a shot?"

"What you guys drinkin'?" she asks.

I answer, "Cuervo."

"Prairie fires?"

A prairie fire is a shot of tequila topped off with Tabasco sauce. It's one of Glenn and my favorite shots. Hell, we even get other people to do it from time to time since the Tabasco sauce kills the tequila's after-taste. I highly recommend trying one some time, especially if you only have cheap tequila to drink.

"No Tabasco," Glenn answers.

"Shitty." she says.

"Not really, we like the taste of straight tequila."

"Speak for yourself!" I exclaim.

Nina laughs as Glenn asks me, "Whaaaa?"

"You heard me."

"Am I the only person who enjoys the taste of good liquor?"

Nina answers, "No! You're just an alcoholic so it's all good to you." She starts playing some music on the computer.

Glenn pours up a shot and asks, "So do you want a shot or not?"

"Hell no!"

He asks me, "Alden?" waving the bottle to tempt me like it's some sorta dog treat.

I gag a little at the sight of it, might've gone a bit overboard. All those shots seem to have my stomach curdling.

I tell him, "Not just yet man," as I hold back my gag reflex, "need to let those last ones settle."

"Aww, you guys are pussies!" he exclaims then takes his shot.

Nina tells him, "Fuck your tequila, I got some vodka in my room if I want to drink some good shit."

"Vodka... vodka is shit... you need some tequila... or scotch... or whiskey."

"Pretty much anything but Vodka?" she asks.

"Yea," Glenn answers, "...Oh, and gin."

I tell him, "I'll take my gin over your fuckin' scotch any day."

"I'll stick with my vodka."

Glenn mutters, "Eh, fuck you both then."

Nina says, "Oh, Glenn, you're so funny." in a tone that conveys, 'Fuck you, you fuckin' drunk.'

There's a short moment of silence that Glenn breaks by telling her, "Play Kevin Spacey's 'Beyond the Sea.'"

"Okay, after this song's done."

"Fuck this song!"

I laugh as Nina says, "Jeez, it's almost fuckin' over."

Feeling increasingly sickly I slowly get up and leave the room taking care not to gag and give away the fact that I am likely about to vomit. Closing the door behind me I cover my mouth and gag with each step as I make my way to the bathroom. As I lock the bathroom door behind me I throw up a little in my mouth filling it with the taste of tequila and the texture of partially chewed ramen noodles. I drop to my knees in front of the toilet and open my mouth letting its contents drizzle out into the toilet. The rancid smell of the puke reaches my nose making me gag again, and throw up a much larger amount. I catch my breath for a moment, and just when I think it's all over I proceed to dry heave for a moment before managing to let out one last vile tasting splash of stomach acid and soda.

Using the toilet handle I help myself to my feet. As the puke swirls away, I shake it off and soak in the feeling of a pleasant Tequila buzz. I wash my face and hands then grab some mouthwash off the counter to sanitize my puke hole with. After swishing it around in my mouth for a moment I spit it into the sink along with a bit of residual phlegm then do the same with some water from the faucet.

Checking the room to make sure everything is back in order I notice a glob of vomit on the floor near the toilet, so I grab a chunk of toilet paper and scoop it up. I toss it in the toilet, flush again, and slip my right shoe off. Catching myself on the sink as I almost tip over—I wipe up the residue the puke left behind with my sock then slip my shoe back on, take a deep breath, wash my hands one last time, and step back into the hallway.

I make my way to the soda fridge in order to get some non-alcoholic fluid back in my system and I am surprised to see that Glenn's parents are back home, sitting there watching TV. Out of habit, I try to walk a little straighter despite the fact that: I'm over 21 and can legally drink, I'm not feeling too drunk having just purged the majority of the liquor from my system, and I kinda stumble around like I'm wasted when I'm completely sober.

Hearing me approach they look my way and say, "Hi," as I walk into the room. I wave hello then grab another soda and a bottle of water from the fridge.

On my way back to the family room I stop to look in the other fridge for some food to help stabilize my stomach in order to avoid having to go another round with the toilet.

I don't think I've ever seen their fridge this empty before!

Normally, this thing is full of leftovers and Glenn's parents try to get me to eat as much as possible since I'm like a human garbage disposal and they don't like to see food go to waste. It's strange that there isn't much in here except the leftovers from his parent's dinner. Out of common courtesy, I don't like to eat anything that they might've brought home with them, because they might actually want it for later. They already supply us with all the soda we can drink and let us raid their fridge whenever we get the munchies, or are just plain hungry, so it'd be real shitty to eat anything they were actually saving for later. I'd feel wrong even asking since they are so generous I'm sure they would say I could have it even if they did want it.

After poking around for a moment, I manage to find some cheese, so I stuff my mouth full and chew it as I slowly make my way back to the family room. I make sure to swallow the last bit before I open the door, a habit I formed in the days that the room was always filled with people and I didn't want to instigate a mass exodus of stoners heading into the kitchen for munchies.

As I walk in and take a seat, Kevin Spacey's rendition of "Beyond the Sea" is playing. I sit down and take a big drink of water before lighting a cigarette.

Logging out of her email, Nina turns away from the computer and asks us, "You guys wanna hear somethin' funny?"

Cracking open my soda, I answer, "Sure."

Glenn says, "It better be quick, I wanna hear this song."

"I think you'll wanna hear this." she tells him.

Glenn ignores her and starts singing along. She looks to me to see if I'm paying attention at least, and I tell her, "Just say it Nina."

"Okay, it just came to me since I saw Mary here with you guys earlier; you won't believe what she asked me to do awhile ago."

I ask, "What was it?" while Glenn hums a few bars to himself.

"She wanted me to have a threesome with her."

"What?!" Glenn asks, snapping out of the song.

Chuckling she repeats, "She wanted me to have a threesome with her and her boyfriend."

I stare at her for a minute in disbelief and she gives me a look that assures me she isn't bull-shitting. I say, "That's fuckin' nuts," then pause in a futile attempt to gather my thoughts before asking, "Didya do it?"

Glenn tries to look like he isn't interested in knowing whether or not his sister had a threesome with Mary, but anything involving Mary or any other red head and sex pulls in his attention as much as it does mine. So much so that he's able to completely tune out the fact that we're talking about his own sister having a threesome.

Nina answers, "I said no."

Glenn asks, "Why?!"

Much like me, he is unable to believe anyone would be able to pass up an opportunity to fuck Mary.

She goes on not answering him, "I guess he didn't even wanna do it, it was her idea."

I exclaim, "Fucking weird!" trying to hold back my laughter.

Glenn exclaims, "Wow!" a few times in disbelief then he quickly grabs the bottle and takes a shot.

At least I'm not the only one who needs a drink at times when it comes to thoughts of Mary.

I spend a moment processing Nina's revelation and trying to find a way to sorta say, 'Thank you for not having a threeway with Mary,' without being blatantly obvious. I look at Nina saying, "That's great Nina." and she laughs when I get up and give her a high-five.

I sit back down as Glenn mutters, "Wow!" to himself one more time before taking another shot and raising the bottle announcing, "Well that's it for the Tequila!"

Wait a second, that was the last of the Tequila?!
I swear there was a lot more left when I last had a shot.
How many did he have while I was throwing up?

The more I look at him, I can see he is looking just like I felt before my trip to the bathroom.
"How the hell is it gone?" I ask, but Glenn pays no attention as he sets the bottle on the table and slouches down on the couch, half conscious. With no more liquor to drink he has immediately lost all interest in the world around him.

As I look back over at Nina she chuckles and asks, "What the hell did you do to him?"

I shrug and say, "I just started hitting the bottle pretty hard after Mary left and apparently he took that as a challenge." Nina laughs as I add, "I'd probably be the same or worse if I hadn't just emptied my stomach in the bathroom."

She points at him and exclaims, "If he pukes I'm not cleaning it up!"

Somehow, Glenn hears that and waves his fist around swinging at thin air and grumbling, "I'm fine... Shut up... I can hold my liquor!"

Nina and I laugh as he settles back down. I tell her, "He'll be fine... you heard the man. Anyway, what's goin' on with you?"

She answers, "Just checking some shit online until I gotta go hang out with Tracy."

"You get to hang out with Tracy, lucky you!"

"Oh yea! She's so fucking annoying! All she does these days is bitch and moan about Ferris this and Ferris that."

You know I've never met two people that call each other best friends who have as much deep-seeded and genuine hatred for each other as Nina and Tracy do. Even mortal enemies have more respect and honor when it comes to dealing with each other then these two. You can't mention one to the other, without some sort of shit talking coming out as a result. I imagine one or the other is always the source of the rumors that often arise about STDs that they may or may not have. Chances are though, if one of them actually has any STDs there's a group of about 50 or so people, including the both of them, that are all infected. Through one person or another they've all slept with each other by proxy at the very least. The people they hang around with cheat on each other and swap boyfriends/girlfriends like they are trying to repopulate a post-apocalyptic world.

"Wait a second!" I point out, "I didn't even think you two were talkin' since her and Ferris hooked up."

She shrugs as I glance at my watch to check the time.

How the fuck is it still this early?

I guess I should head home and try to get something accomplished since Glenn is just passed out for the night.

I get up and start to clean up the room a bit, picking up beer and soda cans. Nina follows suit helping me out, and with our hands full we set them down on the kitchen counter near the sink. With that taken care of we head back into the family room and both look at Glenn who is still in a catatonic state.

Nina asks, "So I take it you're gonna need a ride home?"

"Yea, if you don't mind. If not I can always hoof it."

She says, "I'll give you a ride." when her phone starts beeping. She checks it and says, "I'll be back in a minute." then heads off to her room as she answers the call.

I poke Glenn on the shoulder saying, "Glenn. Glenn! ... Nina's giving me a ride home. You should go lay down in your bed."

He jerks up for a second mumbling, "I can drive." then slouches back down without even opening his eyes.

"No dude, go to bed."

He groans for a moment before falling back asleep..

"Well, suit yourself." I say then turn the TV off, grab my jacket on, and start to leave the room. Before leaving I turn back around, grab the trash can, and put it next to him on the couch so that he has one hand on it. I put a pillow behind his head so he can't lean it back and gargle vomit to the point of drowning in it.

Nina pokes her head in asking, "You ready?"

Putting on my jacket, I answer, "Yea," then looking at Glenn I add, "that'll have to do." before following her out of the room and turning the light off behind me.

Part of me feels kinda bad leaving Glenn like that, but this isn't the first time anyone has done so and in the past it has been done at times that he was in much worse shape.

The garbage can has been half full of his vomit before and on a few occasions we have even had to force him to empty his mouth of the vomit he was gargling. While we do our best to leave each other relatively safe when we're in such conditions, none of us has ever been in the business of babysitting each other, unless absolutely necessary. We've seen each other at our worst, but we still have enough pride not to want to be taken care of, and generally we try to respect that—if at all possible.

I myself have been left passed out in front of my house, on my porch, or on my kitchen floor on multiple occasions—whether it be by Glenn, Ferris, or someone else—and despite some awkward moments being found by my parents, as I'm sure Glenn has had quite a few of himself, I have always been grateful to be left alone in a relatively safe place.

Chapter 21

"Change of Plans"

As she opens the front door Nina tells me, "So, slight change of plans, Ferris is droppin' Tracy off and he volunteered to give you a ride."

"They here right now?"

"Yea."

"Cool."

I follow her outside, closing the door behind me and we walk over to Ferris's car. When we get relatively close Tracy excitedly pops out of the passenger seat.

I say, "Hi Tracy," but she just rushes over to Nina and gives her a big hug without saying a word—leaving me standing there like an idiot. I look over at Ferris and shrug, then quick slip into the car and close the door. We wave goodbye to two of them as we take off.

"So how ya been?" I ask.

"Not too bad, you?"

"Alright."

"Cool."

"What you up to these days?"

"Eh, not too much, been going to the bar a lot, and hangin' out with Tracy."

"That's cool."

"How 'bout you?"

"Not much, same shit as usual."

"Cool."

"It's been a kinda weird day though. Haven't seen much of anyone lately, but I ran into Charlie at school, and both Neil and Mary were over at Glenn's at one point."

"Cool, how's everybody doin'?"

"Eh, Charlie is still a little mopey about everything I guess. Both Mary and Neil seem to be doing alright. And Glenn, well, he's passed out on the couch with the trash can next to him—so nothing's changed there."

Laughing, Ferris asks, "Were you guys drinking Cuervo again?"

"Yea, thought I was keeping up with him pretty well too, but I ended up throwing up and next thing I knew he'd polished off the rest of the bottle."

"Shit."

I crack the window and light a cigarette then say, "So, I gotta ask... I heard through the grapevine that you knocked Tracy up. Is that true?"

"Who told you that?" he asks.

"My mom, but I guess I'm supposed to act surprised when Tracy tells me herself. ... So is it true?"

Hesitating, he admits, "Ye... yeah."

"How you feel about that?"

"Ehhhhhh..." he trails off without even starting a sentence.

I laugh as I tell him, "Enough said."

Ferris sighs then changes the subject asking, "So, I'm goin' to the bar you want me to drop you off at home first or you up for drinkin' some more?"

"I guess I'll go to the bar. I've pretty much recovered after praying to the porcelain gods."

"Cool."

I finish my cigarette and feel the pack to see how many I have left.

Shit, was that the last one?

I tear the pack open and look inside just to be sure.

It was!

I ask Ferris, "Actually, can you just drop me off by the gas station? I need to get some smokes."

"Sure."

After another minute or two of driving Ferris pulls into the gas station near the bar. As I open the door to get out I say, "I'll seeya over there man."

I step out of the car and he asks, "You sure you don't want me to wait?"

"Nah, I could probably use some fresh air before I start drinking again anyways."

"Alright man, I'll seeya shortly then."

I close the door and he pulls off as I head toward the entrance. Two panhandlers stand talking to each other near the door, but I manage to make it inside without having to turn either of them down since they're busy discussing whatever it is panhandlers talk about when they aren't asking for money.

I'd like to think that they even hit each other up for money though. I can imagine them trying to one up each other's sob stories until one of them wins and the loser is forced to go elsewhere to do their begging.

These bastards won't be getting anything from me tonight though; it's not that I'm unsympathetic to people that actually need some help and appreciate what little you can give them, but it's pretty rare that you actually see those people asking for a hand out. The crowd you get around this place just sees you as a mark to con money out of.

One time on his way inside to get a bottle of liquor I saw Glenn give a guy all of the money and change he had on him, which amounted to nearly 20 dollars, and when he came back out the guy tried to hit him up for more. He even got that whole, "Fuck you, asshole!" attitude when Glenn said he didn't have any more cash on him.

And I don't know how many times I've ran into people around here who've supposedly needed money for the train since their car broke down, they locked their keys in it, or some other similarly shitty excuse. They seem to have all taken the same panhandling correspondence course or read the same <u>Panhandling for Dummies</u> book.

Once, I ran into the same guy 3 days in a row. I gave him 5 bucks on the first day, believing that the car he was likely attempting to break into was his and that it had actually broken down. On the 2nd and 3rd days he didn't recognize me, so when he started to give me the same longwinded story I just kept walking and told him he'd already fooled me once.

People like those guys ruin it for all the people who actually desperately need whatever help they can get, but the world doesn't seem to operate on karma or that 'the lord will help you when you need it if you help others when they do' principal, or whatever other philosophy these panhandlers often preach. No, it's fuck the nice guy, give him AIDs, and defecate on his corpse after he's died a slow and agonizing death.

Inside, I wander around a bit looking at snacks for awhile. Nothing seems all that appetizing though, at least none of the immediately consumable items. After combing the isles for a few minutes I manage to find a small bag of cheese curds on the cooled shelves where they keep the sandwiches and whatnot.

Ah, that's one of the best things about the Midwest, or maybe just Wisconsin. I guarantee in most other places you'd probably be pretty hard pressed to find cheese curds at all, let alone find them at a gas station.

I grab the bag and get a pack of cigarettes at the counter then head back outside. Seeing one of the panhandlers greedily eye me as I step out the door I hasten my steps quickly making my way around the side of the building and down the street. Once I'm a safe distance away I stop, open the pack of cigarettes, and light one. In between puffs I nibble on cheese curds as I head toward the bar.

Chapter 22

The Ghost of Pervert Future

Walking around here always reminds me of one of the strangest experiences I've ever had. The night that I met the most perverted person I've ever come into contact with.

At the time I was in a pretty pissy mood about the whole Mary and Ferris getting back together thing; I was bitter at the world in general, but especially the two of them. I had been hanging out with both of them quite a bit before I'd gone to visit my brother in Florida and after coming back I only saw them when we went to Bonnaroo together.

So, I was smoking a cigarette and taking a roundabout way back home from the gas station thinking about killing them both, or somethin' to that effect—maybe a sort of murder frame-up that would leave one dead, and the other suffering for the rest of their life. I was brought back to reality by someone in a truck stopping and saying, "Hey."

Thinking it must've been someone I knew I went up to the passenger window and said, "Hi," as I looked inside to see the driver.

It wasn't anyone I recognized, but he acted as if we were old friends and asked, "So where are all the after-bars?"

"Fuck if I know."

Surprised, he asked, "You aren't headed to one?"

At that point I was figuring that if this was some sort of case of mistaken identity it would resolve itself with one statement. So I told him, "No, I was just heading home after getting some smokes, I'm not even twenty-one so I don't know anything about any after-bars."

He looked puzzled for a second then reached over and opened the door saying, "Here, get in."

Being in a sort of fuck the world, worst case scenario I'm gonna commit a murder in self defense sorta mood, I hopped in. Probably not the smartest choice I've ever made. I guess that whole don't get in a car with strangers thing didn't get absorbed into my subconscious, but I was still racking my brain trying to figure out if the guy was a stranger or just someone I didn't know or remember very well.

As I closed the door I asked, "What's goin' on?"

"So you don't know of any after-bars we could go to?"

"No, I'm only twenty, so I can't get into the bars let alone find out where the after parties are."

"Damn," he said, then after a moment he asked, "You're only twenty?"

"Yea."

Surprised, he looked over at me and said, "Really? You look like you gotta be twenty-five at least."

"Nope, twenty."

At that point a car pulled up behind us and he said, "Oh shit, we better get movin'."

As he started driving I asked him, "So, where we goin'?"

At that point seeing him under the periodic illumination of the street lights I realized that I didn't remember this guy, because I had never met him in my entire life and I didn't know him at all. I started mentally preparing myself for diving out of the car if he was gonna try to take me someplace far away or out in the middle of nowhere and not let me opt to get out and go on my own not-so-merry way. I always did kinda wanna dive out of a moving vehicle like I was in an action movie or somethin'. I checked to make sure nothin' had fallen out of my pockets and casually made sure the door was unlocked as I flicked my cigarette out the window and rolled it up.

"Well," he answered, "I could just drop you off at home, or, you could come over and have a couple drinks. Your twenty, you should be able to drink, even if you can't go out to the bars because of stupid laws."

I thought about it for a second then asked, "Where do you live?" figuring that if I was gonna put myself in a situation I might have to fight my way out of I better not have to run very far to get home. I smoke way too many cigarettes for that shit.

He answered, "Just a couple blocks up the road by the train tracks. How 'bout you?"

"Right over by the junior high."

"Cool, you're not that far away at all."

"Yea."

"We're practicly neighbors."

He slowed down, stopped at the next intersection, and said, "Well this is my street." Then, he asked, "So you wanna stop over and have a couple drinks?"

I thought for a second before answering, "Ehhh, why not, I could use a drink or two."

He said, "Cool. Cool." as he turned the corner.

"I'm not sticking around for very long though."

"That's fine. Well, here we are."

He pulled into his driveway and parked the truck. We both got out and I followed him to the front door.

As he opened the door and took a step inside he said, "Sorry 'bout the mess."

"I'm sure I've seen worse."

After he turned the light on I closed the door.

He opened the fridge and asked, "Wanna beer?"

I answered, "Sure." thinking, 'Good, I'd rather drink somethin' that I opened myself than some drink this guy could've drugged.'

"I got MGD and... let's see..." He shifted around some of the cans in the fridge. "Well, just MGD."

"That's fine."

He handed me a can then holding out his hand he said, "I'm Jeff by the way."

I shook his hand and said, "I'm Alden. Nice to meet you."

"It's nice to meet you too."

With introductions out of the way, we went into his living room and he sat in his chair. I grabbed a seat on the coach and pulled out a cigarette asking, "Can I smoke in here?"

Answering, "Yea, go ahead," he grabbed an ashtray then said, "here you go." as he put it on the coffee table in front of me.

"Thanks."

"No problem."

I lit the cigarette and we bullshitted for a little while before he asked me, "Mind if I put something on to watch?"

"No, go ahead."

The second the tape started playing I knew this guy was a pervert or sexual deviant of some sort and things only got more awkward and strange from there on out. After all, who else in the world would pick up a guy half his age in the middle of the night to have drinks then start playing porn right off the bat as the sole means of entertainment?

Shit, I don't even like watching porn with friends, not one bit, and though Ferris may drunkenly joke about it on occasion I'm pretty sure he's never going to try and rape me. The whole idea of watching porn with other guys has always seemed pretty retarded to me. A bunch of guys sitting around trying to hide the tents they're pitchin' and givin' themselves blue balls isn't my idea of fun at all.

Well, apparently, it wasn't Jeff's idea of fun either, because it didn't take him too long to reach in his pants and start jackin' himself off.

I ignored it at first and just zoned out on the TV, drank my beer, and chain smoked. I don't really know why I didn't just get up and get the fuck out of there the second I realized what he was doing. I think the writer in me wanted an interesting albeit disturbing story to tell while the rest of me was hoping he'd try some shit so I could take out years of pent up aggression by kicking the shit out of this guy. I suppose part of me figured leaving would make me some sort of hypocrite since I've always considered myself somehow more tolerant and open-minded than most people. Mostly though, I think I just wanted to break my normal routine even if it was only for an hour or so and was as disturbing and uncomfortable as this was.

He asked, "Does this make you uncomfortable?"

He knew the answer and seeing as how the sounds of sticky skin on skin friction didn't stop I'm guessing he just wanted me to look at him and watch him jack off, even if it was only for a second.

"Yea, it does."

Standing up he said, "Oh, come on the human body is a beautiful thing, back when I was your age me and my friends used to hang out and have circle jerks all the fuckin' time."

"Wow... times sure have changed."

He went into the kitchen asking, "You need another beer?"

"Yea!"

"Anything else you like to drink? We got liquor."

I thought for a minute and decided to throw out that whole drink shit that couldn't possibly be drugged policy opting for the full of myself logic of, 'Since I'm such a drug god I'd be able to handle anything anyone could throw at me and still remain in control.' Besides it was way too fucked up of a situation to get through on beer alone. So, I asked for the only liquor I could think of at the time, "Yea, you got any Jack Daniel's?"

He looked in the cabinets for a minute then came back into the living room and handed me a beer before setting a shot glass and a half full liter of Jack Daniel's on the table in front of me as he said, "Hear ya go."

He sat back down in his chair, and I poured myself up a shot then lit a smoke before slammin' it.

"So, Jack Daniel's, that's some pretty strong shit."

"Yea."

"I don't know how you can drink that."

"Eh, don't drink it very often, but it's good once in awhile. Had my first shot of it back when I was in grade school. My dad used to pour one up for me every once in awhile when I was little."

"That's cool, personally I can't handle that shit, it's my roommate's bottle." The conversation died out there for awhile until he spoke up saying, "Feel free to jerk off."

"I'll pass on that."

"Ahh, come on, don't be ashamed of your body."

"It's not that I'm ashamed of my body..."

"Then what is it?"

"...it's that I don't want to jerk off in front of another guy."

"Why not? It's not gay or anything."

I beg to differ there, especially when you can't chalk it up to an unavoidable consequence of a bukkake party, but I didn't want to get in some sort of sexual debate.

"Well for one, I find it pretty hard to get aroused when there's another guy around, and more importantly no one's ever seen me naked outside of family members when I was little, and the first time sure as hell ain't gonna be in front of another guy."

Giving up on that he immediately kicked the perversion up a couple notches. Standing up he said, "Well, suit yourself, but I'm going to make myself more comfortable." With that said, he stripped naked and sat back down continuing to jack off.

How this guy could pretty much continuously jack off for so long is a mystery to me, but he presumedly did it from the moment he started till the moment I left, though I could be wrong since I was doing my damndest to tune out the sound of it and never look his way.

Anyhow, after awhile we got to talkin' again.

The saying goes, if life gives you lemons make lemonade, well, if life gives you a naked perverted exhibitionist make...

Make...

Ah, who the fuck am I kiddin'.

I got nothin'.

What I'm getting at though, is that even though this guy didn't give me that previously mentioned opportunity to relieve my pent up aggression, he did give me the perfect opportunity to talk about a lot of things and vent vocally getting a lot of shit out that otherwise might've remained bottled up to this day. In a way, because of that I'm glad I ran into the crazy perve, despite the fact that he creeped the shit out of me and made me feel as if I had been violated in some way.

The great thing about a person you barely know and know you'll most likely never see again is that you can speak freely with them. Especially, when you can look down on them because they are something like...

...let's see...

...some sort of sickening troll-like pervert.

Even if in light of what you tell them they judge you to be a total piece of shit you can just blow them off on account of the fact that they themselves are a piece of shit. Regardless, you can say whatever the fuck you want without having to worry about any consequences, unless of course you put yourself in some sort of position to be blackmailed, but considering the circumstances if anyone was going to do any blackmailing it would've been me, not him.

I vented for awhile about the whole Mary thing and my history with my friend's girlfriends among other things and he gave me the whole you're a good looking guy, nice, smart, personable, you could get yourself a good girl if you just be yourself and be confident speech. I've gotten that speech verbatim from at least ten different people, which makes me really consider there is truth to all those theories of humanity having a shared consciousness. The whole be yourself, and be confident bit has always seemed pretty contradictory for me though, but that's an entirely different rant.

Anyhow, he told me a little about himself too. I'm sure there was some shit that would give a less one-sided picture of him, but I don't remember any of it. The only thing that I remember was a story about how he and his male friends used to jerk off into a cup, and whoever came last had to drink it. Apparently, he would often lose on purpose so he would have to drink the cum. I don't get the point of that game at all. For one, it rewards guys that cum fast, training them to not please their future lovers. More importantly though, it is pretty fucking gay. It rewards the guys who can cum the quickest in front of other guys, not to mention the fact that one guy always ends up drinking his friends' cum.

At one point when I got up to take a leak he insisted that I leave the bathroom door open so he could listen. I humored him and afterwards he repeatedly told me how good I would be at giving golden showers since I'd pissed for so long. After that we switched seats. He suggested this so I would feel more comfortable, but I think he just wanted to be able to look at me more easily. I'm pretty sure of this since at one point when an incredibly hot porn star was on the screen my dick made a single twitch and he immediately said something along the lines of, "Come on, I saw that, you can get aroused around other guys."

Snapping at him I said something like, "Hey, that chick is fuckin' hot! It's not like I'm gettin' off on the fact that you're over their jacking off, and I find it pretty damn weird that you noticed that, because if I was jerking off right now I'd be paying attention to her."

That shut him up pretty quick.

A few minutes later he offered me five bucks to jerk off for him. When I refused he offered ten bucks and when I refused that he offered five for me just to get naked. It'd cost him a fuck load more than a ten spot to get me to jack off for him, but we weren't negotiating and he wouldn't have been able to afford it anyways. He told me he had picked up three people in the same fashion before and all of them took the fiver and jerked off. He was proud of this, especially since two of the three had even blown their loads in his mouth.

I left after that and when he got up to walk me out I caught a glimpse of his tiny penis for the first time. It was hard for me not to burst into laughter. On my way out he asked me to spit in his hand so he'd have some sort of lubrication. So I hacked up the nastiest glob of phlegm I could muster right into his hand, free of charge. If the freak wanted to rub my snotty lung butter on his dick why not let him, at least someone would make use of it.

Looking back on it I think I probably stuck around as long as I did, because I was somewhat simultaneously scared and fascinated by that guy. Fascinated, not so much the guy himself, but the whole idea that such a person manages to exist and survive in this world. Scared, not due to any fear of what he might do or try to do, but by the thought that someone like myself, if given enough time alone, with no real emotional and perhaps more importantly sexual outlet, could someday find themselves trying to get some random stranger to cum in their mouth as if that was as normal of a thing to do as shopping for groceries. The fact that he didn't see anything even remotely homosexual about it makes me think that he was just desperate for any sort of human connection he could get, regardless of the person's gender, and somehow getting another man to cum in his mouth was the best he could hope to achieve.

What the hell happened in his life that it came to that?

Whatever it was, it is something that we should all certainly avoid.

Ugh!

Somehow even thinking about it makes me feel dirty.

In order to cleanse my mind of that memory, I take a long drag off my cigarette burning it down well into the filter. Exhaling with a deep sigh, I flick the butt into the street then quickly kill off the remainder of the cheese curds and toss the empty bag in the trash can outside the bar.

Chapter 23

Gin and...

Upon walking into the bar I am greeted by the usual doorman, Evan, who is also my sister's boyfriend at the moment.

I can't say I really approve of him dating my sister, but she seems to be happy so I have no intention of getting in the way of that. He's an alright guy, but he's too much of a party animal and he's one of those people that is always trying to be the center of attention. He can be fun to party with at times since there is never a lack of interesting occurrences and excitement around him, but I imagine even his best friends have probably had a thought along these lines, 'He's a great guy, but I'd never want him dating my sister.'

It doesn't help that when I first heard about him years ago it was severely muffled by my sister's tears. Apparently, she had gone home with him after bar one night and he had stripped naked in his living room expecting sex then grabbed her by the wrist in an attempt to stop her from leaving. I imagine after seeing the fear in her face he let go, and she went home in tears as if he had actually tried to rape her. For the longest time after that she referred to him as "Evan the asshole."

When I first met him I actually introduced myself drunkenly saying, "Hey you're Evan the Asshole. I'm Alden, Anita's brother." He eyed me suspiciously for a moment before I told him, "I don't mean any offense... some of my best friends are assholes." It took him a minute to realize who I was and that I wasn't trying to start shit, but we ended up having a drink and never had any real problems with each other. Years later now, they have gotten over that initial "misunderstanding" as she would call it. They started dating each other awhile ago and she no longer refers to him as "Evan the Asshole," but a large part of me will always identify him as such.

That said, I don't know whether or not he's good for my sister, but I must say one last thing on the subject of Evan. No man should ever have to see someone wave around an uncircumcised penis that has been inside his sister. Unfortunately though, on one night that he was black-out drunk, I was subjected to such trauma in the back patio of the bar; there are some things you just can never unsee.

Extending a hand he asks "Hey! How's it goin'?"

I shake his hand and say, "I'm alright, pretty drunk, but doin' alright. How 'bout you?"

He laughs and says, "Pretty much the same," then puts a hand on my shoulder and tells me, "you might wanna take it easy, you're already looking pretty ragged."

Looking around I see that it's a pretty slow night at the bar; not too many people are there aside from a small group by Ferris, who is playing pool, my sister who sits talking with a couple of friends, and a couple people sitting at the bar talking to Henry, the bartender.

Taking it easy is probably not in the cards with him behind the bar.

I pat Evan on the back and say, "I'll try," then starting to walk away I add, "might be hard though with Henry pouring the drinks." Evan laughs as I head over to the bar.

Henry notices me and breaks away from the group of people talking at the end of the bar. Seeing that I'm already half in the bag he strokes his beard and smiles asking, "Gin and Tonic?"

I lean against the bar to brace myself since standing still is seeming somewhat problematic at the moment then answer, "Of course."

He pours up the drink, which is pretty much just a glass of gin on the rocks with a tiny splash of tonic then says, "I'm surprised to see you. You're sister said you weren't coming out tonight."

Shrugging I tell him, "I wasn't really planning on, but the Tequila ran dry, and Glenn passed out. So, here I am."

"Tequila?!... and here I thought you didn't drink anything but Gin... and maybe the occasional bomb."

"I try not to mix too many things out in public."

Setting my drink on the bar in front of me, he laughs and says, "Now where's the fun in that?"

I hand him $5 and say, "There might not be much fun in it, but I try to keep myself from going off the deep end. That happens way more than I would like as it is."

"I like seeing you wasted though, it's funny, and it's good to see you break outta your shell."

I shrug as he hands me $3 back and I give him a bill asking, "Can I get a buck in quarters?"

He grabs the dollar saying "Sure."

I put the other $2 on the bar for a tip and bend the straw over the side of my glass before taking a drink. Henry hands me the 4 quarters and I say, "Thanks."

As I start to turn away he stops me saying, "Hey, don't go anywhere just yet. You're doing a shot with me."

I set my drink on the bar after taking another sip then light a cigarette as he pulls out a couple of shot glasses and grabs the bottle of Maker's Mark.

Oh god! Most of my worst nights of drinking end with a shot of Maker's.

As he pours the shots I say, "You know you're gonna be the death of me."

He laughs, lifts his shot, and says, "Cheers."

I pick up my shot and clink it against his saying, "Cheers."

We down the shots and I grimace for a second before saying, "Thanks," and taking a big drink of gin.

He says, "No problem." and heads over to someone further down the bar who needs another drink.

I head over to my sister's table where she is sitting with a couple of friends. She greets me saying, "Hey Alden! I didn't think you were coming out."

"Eh, Glenn passed out after we finished a bottle of tequila we had, so I hitched a ride with Ferris."

"Cool."

I set my drink on the table and tell her, "Watch this for a second." then quick put a quarter down on the pool table.

Ferris looks up from his shot and says, "Nice, I can't remember the last time we played."

"Yea, it's been awhile... don't go losing on me."

He says, "I won't." as he takes the shot and makes it.

Heading back over by my sister, I say, "Nice one."

I post up at the end of my sister's table and grab my drink then alternate between nervously puffing on my cigarette and sipping my drink as she talks with her friends for awhile. I try to follow the conversation and see if I have anything to add to it, but between my drunkenness and their fast paced rambling I am unable to even get a grasp of what they are talking about let alone find a place to add anything to the conversation. This only speeds up the pace of my drinking and chain smoking.

After awhile, having fallen out of the conversation herself, one of the girls tells/asks me, "You know your sister is beautiful?"

I look at her for a second trying to muster up what the hell kind of response a normal person would give to that, but I come up empty, so instead I just make a pathetic attempt to flirt with her by raising an eyebrow and saying, "You know some people say we look alike."

What the fuck just came outta your mouth?

I don't know! It sure wasn't my foot though.

That's about as far from a normal response as anyone could've given. If I didn't know any better I would think you are actively trying to be weird and creepy.

The obviously confused, awkward, and almost embarrassed for me look on the girl's face pretty much says it all—so I give her an nervous smile, raise my glass,

slam down what's left of the drink, and get another one
from Henry.

I have no delusions that I will ever pick any girl up
from this bar, but that was exceptionally pathetic. While a
bar close to home that your family members often frequent
can be an awesome and fun place, almost an extension of
home itself, it is a horrible place to try to meet any
potential romantic partners, especially when the family
members in question are your sister and mother. When
anyone you might find attractive or like has already met
and/or befriended your mother and sister, you are doomed
from the get go to be looked at more like a little brother
than anything else. Yet despite the fact that they have
unknowingly destroyed any chance you might've had in
the first place they will try to encourage you and get your
hopes up regarding these same girls.

Who am I kidding though, even if that wasn't the case,
no girl in her right mind would go home with a guy that
can't even drive, in order to hang out with him in his
parent's basement. Shit, even the majority of girls in a
"wrong" mind wouldn't be that desperate, but there is
probably far more to my consistently striking out than just
that. In fact, I'm sure that there is.

Afterall, Anita was able to hook up our brother with
her first girlfriend at one point and he even ended up
taking her home to our parent's basement. I remember this
distinctly, because I spent the better portion of a few
nights sitting in silence on my porch or sleeping on the
floor or a chair somewhere in the house having been
kicked out of my own room so the two of them could have
sex for hours in my bed. It was a good thing that the

majority of the futon was covered by the cushion from a large papasan chair that Glenn had broken in a drunken stupor one night, because due to what was described to me as a "geyser" of female ejaculate the cushion was drenched and needed to be thrown away but the mattress itself had been saved from ruin.

After I get my drink, which is somehow even stronger than the first one, I return to the table lighting another cigarette. As I get there my sister gets up and grabs her jacket off one of the hooks on the wall. Then, through a series of signals and a roll call of sorts a few other people throughout the bar get up and start quickly making their way out the back door.

As Anita puts her jacket on she tells me, "Were going out back to get high, you're welcome to join us."

I say, "Cool, I'm down." and fall in line behind her, joining the small caravan of people heading out back.

Ferris holds out his arms by the pool table as this development has stopped his game in its tracks. He tells his opponent, "Come on man. The game was almost over." but this falls on deaf ears as they walk out the door. Passing the table, I check the quarters to see if my game is coming up and he tells me, "You're up next, if we can ever finish this game."

I check my watch and see that bar close is approaching, "Shit! Well, hopefully we can get a full game in."

He sighs saying, "Yea," then finishes his drink and heads off to get another one as I make my way outside.

Chapter 24

No Need for Introductions

Being the last person out the door I close it behind me as everyone forms a circle. There are 7 or so people including my sister and myself. One of the guys pulls out a pipe and quickly packs some weed in it then takes a hit hit and passes it to his left. Another guy on the other side of the circle does the same.

Before taking a hit off the pipe that has made into her hands my sister asks one of the guys supplying the weed, "You've met my brother before, right?"

We both look at each other skeptically as we seem to recognize one another, but can't be certain we have ever officially met as we don't remember the each others' names.

"I think so..." he stammera.

"I'm not sure." I say.

"We probably were drunk when we did," he adds.

"Yea." I agree.

Anita hits the pipe and hands it to me then letting her hit out she gestures to us saying, "Well, Alden this is Jon... Jon, Alden."

He nods to me saying, "Nice to meet you again."

Before hitting the pipe I say, "Nice to meet you," then I pass it on adding, "Maybe we'll remember meeting this time."

He laughs and raises his drink saying, "I think the odds are probably against us. Cheers!"

I say, "Cheers." and we clink our glasses together before we both take big swigs. He sets his drink down on a nearby table as one of the pipes makes it around to him.

For the sake of not over complicating the fuck out of things, the bowls make their way around the rotation normally and they do so at an unusually fast speed since no one seems inclined to stand out in the cold to get high for longer than they have to.

I've never cared all that much for smoking more than one bowl at once, because unless you have an incredibly huge group of people, it's just fucking confusing as hell. Thankfully, these guys were smart enough not to try and send the pipes in opposite directions, because usually some asshole thinks that's a great idea. Then, people get screwed over having to hit two pipes at once and eventually the pipes both end up going in the same direction anyways.

One time due to a malfunctioning lighter, one of those crappy see-thru ones that always either crack open or the wheel flies off almost taking out someone's eye, I ended up with four pipes in my hands and had to have people light them for me two at a time. After that, we had two sets of two pipes going in rotation together until someone had enough sense to hit one and wait a moment before hitting the other and passing it on.

Once the bowl he packed is cashed the guy Anita introduced me puts it in his coat pocket and slams the remainder of his drink saying, "Well, I gotta get goin'."

He gives her a hug and she says, "It was good to see you, you need to come out more often."

I step out of his way to give him a clear path to the door and he shakes my hand saying, "It was nice meeting you again Alden."

As he heads back into the bar I say, "It was nice meeting you... too."

I've already forgotten his name.

I hate meeting people at the bar! Unless you end up sitting down and bullshitting for the better part of the night you are sure to forget each other and always have to go through that same awkward reintroduction the next time you "meet."

It doesn't help that my sister knows pretty much 90% of the people that come in this place. At one point or another I've gotten a passing introduction to the majority of them, but very rarely have I actually had the chance to talk and get to know anyone. Often I have found myself bombarded with introductions to anywhere from 5 to 20 people back to back and very few have ever stuck, unless there is an attractive girl among them, but even then I'm usually too fucking drunk and/or high to really remember them the next day, let alone the next time we see each other.

I can't really blame anyone forgetting me either, because most of those same factors are likely in play for them as well. Also, there is the fact that I generally do not leave a good or even memorable first impression on people. I am the type of person that grows on you over time rather than someone who you can instantly tell if you will get along with. At my best I am not likeable at first, except maybe in some really rare cases when there is some sorta cosmic alignment. No, at my best I am forgettable; then, over time people gradually begin to like me so subtly that they don't even realize that wasn't always the case. At my worst, when people first meet me they tend to suspect that I have some sort of retardation or mild autism.

Once the remaining bowl is cashed its owner asks, "Is everybody good? Or should I pack another one?"

Everyone looks at each other weighing whether or not smoking more would be worth standing out in the cold any longer. One person says, "I'm good, it's too damn cold." and everyone else echoes the sentiment. We all head inside as quickly as we came out.

Chapter 25

An Unfinished Game

As we all file back into the bar Evan makes his way to the door. He checks to make sure no one was left outside then picks up a wooden board leaning against the wall and bars the door with it so no one can go out there anymore. I grab a stool near the pool table as Ferris's opponent quickly sets his beer down, takes his jacket off, and grabs the cue he was using.

Ferris tells him, "I didn't leave ya much:"

He eyes the table for a moment before saying, "Jesus you're fuckin' right!" He shrugs then quickly makes a half-assed attempt at a bank shot barely managing to nick the ball he was going for. This leaves Ferris in position to finish the game without any complications.

Ferris gets up off his stool and grabs his cue saying, "Not a bad try."

His opponent groans, "Eh," and he makes his way back to his beer to takes a big swig.

I tell Ferris, "Finish him off man."

"I'll try."

As Ferris sinks the first of the two stripes left on the table I grab my usual cue from its resting place in the corner. I am one of the few people that use it due to its beat up appearance, the fact that it isn't a full-size cue, (which is actually helpful considering the tables placement in relation to the walls of the room and the dart-machine), and the strange bulge in the shaft that somehow makes it look misshapen when it's actually among the straightest of the cues that the bar has. I examine the tip to make sure it hasn't been broken off since the last time I used it then grab the chalk off the table and lightly dust it.

Ferris eyes his next shot and looks back at me saying, "Excuse me," since I'm directly in his way.

I get up and shuffle along the wall while setting the chalk back on the edge of the table. He takes his shot and easily makes the last of the stripes leaving himself with an easy shot on the 8 ball, which sits right in front of the side pocket.

"Nice!" I tell him as I grab my drink.

Ferris quickly rounds the table and tells his opponent, "Looks like this is it."

Looking at the table, his opponent exclaims, "Shit!"

Ferris lines up the shot and tells him, "Side pocket."

Before he even takes the shot his opponent says, "Good game."

Ferris makes the shot, but comes dangerously close to scratching in the process. His opponent's face lights up for a brief second, but he bows his head in shame when the cue ball comes to a stop just short of the corner pocket.

They shake hands and both say, "Good game."

Returning his cue to the rack the defeated tells Ferris, "You're pretty good, but I'll getcha next time." He finishes his drink before adding, "Time for me to call it a night though. Have a good one."

Ferris says, "You too." and the guy heads off.

I take a swig from my drink and set it down before taking my quarter off the table and another two of them out of my pocket. Ferris sets the rack on the table, hooking in the remaining balls with it. I put my quarters in and force the table's sticky mechanism to accept them by thrusting it in with the bottom of my cue. I polish off my drink and start to fill the rack with the rest of the balls from under the table.

Finishing his drink, Ferris asks, "You want another one?"

I say, "Sure." and finish racking the balls as he grabs my glass before hurrying off to the front of the bar.

With all the balls in place I set the rack by the rest of the cues, sit down, and light another cigarette. After a moment, I hear Henry call out, "Last call!"

Ferris hurries back and hands me a drink saying, "He poured it really strong."

I shrug and tell him, "I don't think it's possibly for it to be any stronger than the last one. Well, unless it isn't gin in here."

Ferris laughs and sets his drink down then grabs his cue saying, "We're gonna have to make this quick."

"Yea," I agree.

I get up and take a big drink as he breaks. He sinks a solid and a stripe on the break and takes a quick drink as he surveys the table to find his best option. He takes stripes and makes a couple more balls before missing a shot. I take another drink before taking my shot and making a solid. I don't leave myself in very good position for the next shot, but somehow I almost manage make a difficult bank shot.

Ferris says, "Nice try," as he scrambles into position to take his next shot. Then, just as he is about to shoot his cell phone rings. He stops saying, "Damn it!" then answers his phone, "Heeey! ... I'm almost done. ... They just called last call. ... I'm playing pool with Alden... Yea. ... I'll call you back in a minute when I'm on my way. ... Bye" He hangs up and lets out a big sigh as he looks at me and says, "Fucking women!"

"Tracy?" I ask.

He rolls his eyes saying, "Yea,"

As I lift my drink to take a swig I say, "Good times."

Having been completely thrown off his game by Tracy he misses an easy shot and grumbles, "God damn it!" as he grabs his drink.

I set my drink down and take a drag off my cigarette while I line up my shot.

Ferris says, "You know I think you have the right idea being single and not getting mixed up in all that bullshit."

I make the shot then tell him, "Eh, it's not really a choice that I've made, I'm just horribly unlucky in that department."

"We're all unlucky when it comes to women, just in different ways."

I nod saying, "Fair enough," then round the table stopping along the way to take a quick drink before adding, "for me it's a little different than most though..."

As I line up my shot he asks, "How so?"

I look up at him to say, "You guys make a sort of compromise, you get sex or companionship or love or whatever and in exchange you have to put up with the negative aspects of a relationship as well. I on the other hand am in a sorta perpetual limbo: I don't have to deal with the bullshit, but I don't get to experience the good parts either." I look back down and take my shot miscuing horribly.

Ferris gets up saying, "Yea, but you're free."

I take a drink as he makes a ball then tell him, "Yea, but it's hard to really explain. ... It's kinda like being the only free person left in the world, yet being jealous of everyone, because the only reason you're free is that no one sees enough value in you to make you their slave."

Ferris tilts his head and sort of nods as if to say that he gets want I mean. He makes another shot then pauses to take a quick drink. Suddenly, Evan comes in the back and starts knocking the remaining balls on the table into the pockets. Ferris and I both ask, "What the hell man?!"

"Bars closin', everybody's gotta go."

"Shit!"

We both slam the rest of our drinks and grab another empty or two to set down up front on our way out. After we put the empty drinks on the bar Ferris asks me, "You want a ride?"

"Nah, it's only a couple blocks."

"Alright man."

We both do the handshake and say, "Seeya man." then Ferris rushes off pulling out his phone to call Tracy.

I walk over to my sister and ask, "You headin' home, or are you hangin' out with Evan?"

"I'm goin' with Evan."

"Cool, well, I'll see you tomorrow then."

"Goodnight."

"Goodnight."

I head out of the bar saying, "Seeya Henry."

He calls out, "Take it easy Alden."

Chapter 26

Into the Gutter

Outside the bar, the cold air hits me and I start to really feel the effects of all the alcohol in my system. I lean against the building and light a cigarette as I watch the few people that stayed till bar close rush off to their cars. One couple stumbles to the restaurant across the street to get some food and coffee in order to sober up a bit before driving home. I space out for a moment contemplating getting some food myself until the electric beer sign behind me turns off; I take that as my cue to leave. Buttoning up my jacket, I head down the sidewalk in the general direction of my house.

Down the road a ways, I pass a couple making out in the alley by another bar.

God, I want that!
Why can't I have that?
What the hell am I missing?
I wonder if Mary could tell me.
Fuck!
Why the fuck can't I just get her out of my goddamn head?

It's not like I'm holdin' on to that retarded hope that we will eventually end up getting together, because we are soulmates or some bullshit.

Hey, at least you didn't make a total ass outta yourself like the last few times.

Yeah, that's a fuckin' miracle too considerin' we were drinkin' Cuervo.

Yeah, no hangin' all over her, no futile not to mention horrible hitting on her, didn't even say something as fucked up as...

Efuckinough with that shit! Remembering that will only make me feel even worse about myself.

Is that even possible?

I sure as hell hope not!

I flick my cigarette into the road and mumble to myself, "God damn it! Fuckin' mother fuck, fuck. Fuck!" I start to stumble across the street heading away from my house and toward the lake. Forgetting about the median I catch it with my foot and fall onto my stomach on the other side of the street. I quietly snicker to myself for a moment and it slowly turns into a loud psychotic laugh as I roll over onto my back—making no effort to get up and out of the road. I turn my head to the side and hack out a bit of phlegm brought up by the cold air then light another cigarette and stare up at the sky as I smoke.

Maybe I'm not missing anything.

You know, I'm not sure when it happened, but I've turned out to be a pretty fucking horrible person, I don't really deserve any happiness in my life.

I'm a horrible grandson, rarely visiting except to get a fuckin' hair cut.

I'm even more horrible of a great-grandson, Dean has visited the old broad more than me and he's only lived here for one out of the last seven years. She probably ain't got too many years left either.

I'm a horrible son. I don't talk to my dad that often except when we go to the shooting range or pool hall and out to eat every once in awhile. Half the time he tries to get me to sit with him and talk in the living room I'm too busy formulatin' an exit strategy to pay much attention to what we're or more accurately he's talkin' about. He's provided me with room and board my entire life. He's given me spending cash that I've blown on drugs and other crap. He's given me computers, games, and movies—but I don't express my appreciation for any of that aside from a, "Thanks dad," that regardless of how sincere it is, doesn't sound like it is at all. Instead, I just end up ignoring the bastard more dedicating my time to the things he's given me.

My mom on the other hand I'm even worse to. Not that I'm mean or an asshole to her, but I'm too self-involved to spend any time with her. At times I don't even turn to look and acknowledge her existence when she comes to say, "Hi," to me.

It's not that I don't love these people, whatever that means. It's just that I often tend to be a selfish prick and I don't really seem to consider others very often. Sure, at times I can be a great listener and try my damnedest to help people solve their problems, but to be completely honest more often than not it's done with selfish ulterior motives. Maybe it's just to satisfy my own curiosity, to laugh on the inside about someone else's problems, or that I kinda enjoy watching people sabotage their own lives—but more often than not I only pretend to truly give a shit.

Who else but a fucking horrible friend would be so selfish as to try to steal away their friends' girlfriends as frequently as I have?

And what the fuck kind of friend has a deep seeded hatred for most of the people that would call him their friend?

Shit, the entirety of my being seems to be founded around a sort of lazy malevolence toward everyone and everything that I come into contact with!

Hearing a car, I tilt my head to get a better look and see headlights headed my way.

Maybe I should just let this bastard run me over.
Being dead would make life a lot easier.
Come on now, get out of the road. You have never been one to commit suicide, you get too much of a masochistic enjoyment out of your own suffering.
I suppose you're right, it's sorta my own self-imposed penance.

I look at the headlights approaching one last time then log roll toward the curb.

I wonder if this is why they teach us the log roll in elementary school gym class. By teaching it to us at such a young age we have this simple seemingly useless skill ready to use without thinking in occasions like this.

I crack my head on the curb and come to a stop in the gutter then rub the back of my head and check my hand for blood as the road lights up when the car zooms by.

I take the last drag off my cigarette, which was miraculously unharmed during my roll, and mutter to myself, "I'm tired of this shit."

It's the same crap over and over every god damn day with only an inconsequential variation here and there. It's like I'm Bill Murray in <u>Groundhog Day</u> without the luxury of having the ability to correct my mistakes. Shit, even learning from them is virtually impossible!

I have to find a way out of this routine I'm stuck in or one of these days someone's gonna come up to me and say something like, "Hi," or, "What's up?" and I'm just gonna snap and make for their eyeballs with the nearest pointy object I can get my hands on, or maybe I'll just crack their skull open and start eating their brains. Shit, at least jail, or more likely a stay in an asylum would be a welcome change of pace!

But won't that just lead to another routine?

Yea, I suppose it would.

And for that matter is it even possible to avoid getting stuck in one routine or another?

Well, I suppose I could make a routine out of constantly changing routines, but even that would ultimately just be like any other routine. Maybe I should've let that fuckin' car run me over. Though ultimately even the afterlife would be composed of some sort of routine: whether it be constantly bowing before god waiting for your turn to give him fellatio so you can finally be filled with his great essence, being raped by demons, or suffering through the routines of your next life. Even if there's only nothingness after death that's a routine in itself. The only upside with that is there would be no way to know it.

I pull out another cigarette and light it.

It's this fucking city that really gets to me though. I'm just stuck here suffocating on my own failings. I've tried to escape with videogames and movies and drugs and anime and all the possible combinations of them, but those are just temporary fixes. Once the liberating feeling they give me wears off I just end up hating the everyday shit even more.

I close my eyes and roll over resting my head on the curb.

I gotta get the fuck out of here, or I'll be stuck here hating my life until the day I die and possibly beyond it.

There's gotta be someplace out there that even I can enjoy.

My eyes are opened by a burning sensation in my hand. I look down at the cigarette smoldering in between my fingers and fling it into the road.

I really hope there's at least someplace better than this out there.

Just as I'm about to nod off again I feel a snowflake land on my face. I roll onto my back and stare up at the flurries of lake-effect snow as they float down dusting me and everything else. Closing my eyes I feel them land and melt on my face...